EllRay Jakes
the Recess King!

BY **Sally Warner**

ILLUSTRATED BY
Brian Biggs

PUFFIN BOOKS
An Imprint of Penguin Group (USA)

PUFFIN BOOKS

Published by the Penguin Group

Penguin Group (USA) LLC

375 Hudson Street

New York, New York 10014

USA * Canada * UK * Ireland * Australia* New Zealand * India * South Africa * China

penguin.com

A Penguin Random House Company

Published simultaneously in the United States of America by Viking Children's Books and Puffin
Books, imprints of Penguin Young Readers Group, 2015

LIBRARY OF CONGRESS CATALOGING-IN-PUBLICATION DATA

Warner, Sally, date– author.

EllRay Jakes the recess king! / by Sally Warner ; illustrated by Brian Biggs.

pages cm.—(EllRay Jakes)

Summary: Eight-year-old EllRay Jakes of Oak Glen Primary School is looking
for a new best friend, and he decides that the best way to find one is to come up with
a bunch of amazing things to do at recess—and see who shares in the fun.

ISBN 978-0-451-46911-3 (hardcover)

1. African American boys—Juvenile fiction. 2. Best friends—Juvenile fiction. 3. Friendship—Juvenile
fiction. 4. African American families—Juvenile fiction. 5. Elementary schools—Juvenile fiction.
6. Oak Glen (Calif.)—Juvenile fiction. [1. African Americans—Fiction. 2. Best friends—Fiction.
3. Friendship—Fiction. 4. Family life—Fiction. 5. Schools—Fiction.] I. Biggs, Brian, illustrator.
II. Title. III. Series: Warner, Sally, date– EllRay Jakes.

PZ7.W24644Eo 2015   813.54—dc23 [Fic]   2014043907

Puffin Books ISBN 978-0-14-751252-9

Printed in the United States of America

7   9   10   8   6

A SPARE FRIEND

"Okay. Now that I think about it, maybe none of these five guys is *perfect*, but like I said about Nate, I can fix that. All I have to do is to hang out with them more, get to know them better. Starting tomorrow morning.

And then I can choose which kid I want to be my spare friend.

Who will it be? Major, Marco, Nate, Jason, or Diego?

Maybe the winner can even become *my* personal assistant someday! I know Corey's way too busy winning swim meets and polishing his medals to take on that role, even if he would. But having a personal assistant does sound pretty cool.

Now, all I need is to figure out who the lucky kid will be.

It would be great to have a new friend by Friday, the day of Alfie's show. But my long-term goal is to have one by the end of this month.

January.

Then I'll have a happy new year for sure!

BOOKS BY SALLY WARNER

* * *

THE ELLRAY JAKES SERIES

EllRay Jakes Is <u>Not</u> a Chicken!

EllRay Jakes Is a Rock Star!

EllRay Jakes Walks the Plank!

EllRay Jakes the Dragon Slayer!

EllRay Jakes and the Beanstalk

EllRay Jakes Is Magic!

EllRay Jakes Rocks the Holidays!

EllRay Jakes the Recess King!

THE EMMA SERIES

Only Emma

Not-So-Weird Emma

Super Emma

Best Friend Emma

Excellent Emma

To Todd Warner, best brother ever! —S.W.

•••

For Liam, Recess King of Penn Wynne —B.B.

CONTENTS

★ ★ ★

THE TERRIBLE TRUTH

"What's so great about going to the grand opening of the park tomorrow?" I ask my sister Alfie, as I make a snow angel on her fluffy bedroom rug. "So they fixed it up a little. It will still be the same old boring place."

My name is EllRay Jakes, and I am eight years old. I know this kind of stuff.

"Nuh-uh," four-year-old Alfie argues, scowling. "It said 'new' on the sign in the post office, didn't it? And signs don't lie. It's against the law. There's gonna be fwee hot dogs, Mom said, so we each get to ask a fwend."

"*Fwee*" means "free" in Alfie-speak. And "*fwend*" means "friend." Alfie's r's sort of come and go.

I sigh. "A park's not new just because they plant better grass, and change the benches so people can't sleep on them, and paint over the graffiti. Dad said that's all they were going to do. And it's January, Alfie. It might be raining."

"But there's probably a better play area now," Alfie says, ignoring my weather forecast.

The old play area at Eustace B. Pennypacker Memorial Park only had one swing set, and one tetherball pole that has been missing its actual ball for almost a year, I remind myself. So it would be hard to make the play area any *worse*.

"Listen, Alfie," I say. "We already saw the so-called new park the other day, didn't we? When Mom got lost on the way to Trader Joe's? We drove right by it."

Our mom sometimes goes a different way to the store when traffic gets too crowded. She also likes to park our Toyota with plenty of space on each side, even though the car is older than I am.

Mom is a very careful driver.

I am going to have the coolest car *ever*, when I grow up! It will always be new, and it will have flames painted on the sides. Or at least skinny stripes.

"But when we saw the park, it didn't have a wibbon in fwont of it for our queen to cut with giant scissors, *EllWay*," Alfie says, as if I have just missed the most obvious point about Oak Glen's newest old park, which is opening tomorrow morning, like I said. Saturday.

"EllWay" is Alfie's version of "EllRay," which is a shorter—and less awful—version of "Lancelot Raymond," my full, official name.

My mom writes love stories for ladies, see, about dead or imaginary kings and queens. I guess she got a little carried away naming me when I was born. Moms sometimes do that, in my opinion. And my college professor dad was probably too busy studying weird rocks to put up an argument.

Later, as time went by, my too-fancy name was shortened first to L. Raymond, and then to L. Ray.

But now, everyone just calls me EllRay.

And I won't do much more translating for Alfie, I promise.

"This is California, Alfie," I remind her. "Oak Glen doesn't *have* a queen. That lady you're talking about is our new mayor. She just *acts* like a queen."

The new mayor shows up everywhere, wearing a fancy hat. It is the only ladies' hat in Oak Glen, I think. She also waves a lot.

I try not to sigh again as I click my robotic insect action figure—already cool enough!—into a deadly-looking tank. I start rolling it toward the lavender pony whose long blond tail Alfie is combing. I imagine destroying its golden corral.

C–R–R–R–U–N–C–H!

Nothing personal, lavender pony.

"That lady *is too* the queen," Alfie informs me. "Just because she doesn't wear her queen-hat all the time," she adds, shaking her own head so hard that her three soft, puffy braids swing back and forth. "You probably think she should wear it to bed, don't you?" she continues. "Or when she goes swimming? But real queens don't do that. I asked Mom once, and she said no. So, *hah*."

Alfie has recently discovered sarcasm, I am sorry to say.

"You're mixing stuff up," I tell her. "First, it's called a crown, not a 'queen-hat,'" I begin. "And second—"

But Alfie has moved on. "You don't *have* anyone to invite to the park," she interrupts. "Because you're running out of fwends."

I feel my cheeks get hot, because what Alfie just

said is basically the terrible truth. And I'm her big brother, and she needs to look up to me! "What? I am not running out of friends," I argue, but I don't sound very convincing.

"Well, I have Suzette, Arletty, and Mona to choose from," Alfie says, setting aside her star-spangled horse to argue with me. "And you just have Corey, only he's always busy swimming."

My best friend, Corey Robinson, is an eight-year-old swimming champion. He will probably be in the Olympics some day, everyone says.

I don't know what his plans are after that. Neither does he. His parents haven't told him yet.

"I have other friends, too," I tell Alfie. "What about Kevin?"

Kevin McKinley is the only other boy with brown skin in Ms. Sanchez's third grade class at Oak Glen Primary School, in Oak Glen, California. He has been one of my two best friends for a couple of years. But lately, he's been hanging out a lot with a couple of kids who live on his street, but who go to private school. I don't even know their names.

It's too risky for me to ask Kevin to come to the park tomorrow, even though he really, really likes hot dogs. He might say no! Or he could tell the other guys in our class that it's babyish for an eight-year-old to care about a new play area in some lame new-old park.

And then our friendship would really be over.

"I thought you said Kevin was sometimes *Jared's* fwend now," Alfie says.

Jared Matthews, my part-time enemy.

"I never told you that," I object. "Anyway, it changes around. And since when do you keep track of my life? Mind your own business, Alfie. You've got enough problems."

"You need a spare fwend," Alfie tells me, ignoring what I just said about problems. "You know," she says, grabbing another horse to brush. "The way Mom's car has a spare tire."

Both of us were in my mom's car last week when it got a flat tire on San Vicente Street, which is always super busy. Mom steered our wobbling car over to the side of the road. She told us to stay put while she called for help. But it was scary, waiting in the backseat as all that traffic whizzed by. I pretended it wasn't scary, though, because of Alfie.

I look out for her—in secret.

The spare tire that the auto club guy put on our car looked like it belonged to a clown car, it was so little. I was embarrassed for our poor Toyota.

I don't want a spare *friend* like that!

I'm already the smallest kid in my class, aren't I? I could use someone big.

"*You* know," Alfie continues. "A spare. For emergencies, like this one."

"For your information, *Alfie,* going to Penny-packer Park for a free hot dog isn't an emergency," I tell her, getting to my feet.

Alfie and her goofy opinions can just stay here playing with sparkly fake horses, I tell myself. I am trying to ignore the voice in my head that is saying she's a little bit right.

"You should hold an audition," Alfie announces before I can escape. "That's what we're doing at *my* school. It was all Miss Nancy's idea."

Alfie goes to Kreative Learning and Daycare, even though they spell "creative" wrong, which drives my dad bonkers. "You're auditioning friends at daycare?" I ask, tossing in a little sarcasm of my own.

"No," Alfie says, calm as anything. "We auditioned for our spring show last week. The best part of the show is called *Brown Bear, Brown Bear.* And I'm gonna be the *star.* Mom already started making my costume."

"You're the bear?" I ask, my forehead wrinkling. Because usually, Alfie is more of a kitty or a bunny or a sparkling pony kind of girl.

She might make an exception if she could be a panda, but Ms. Sanchez says pandas aren't really bears. Anyway, they're black and white, not brown.

"I'm the *goldfish*," she says, sighing at having to explain something so simple. "I want to be the last animal everybody sees, so I'll get all the clapping. I figured it out."

"Good luck with that," I call over my shoulder as I leave Alfie's pink and purple palace. I mean room.

"At least I have *fwends*!" Alfie yells after me.

✳ **2** ✳

MY POSSIBILITIES

Okay, so I went to the grand re-opening of Eustace B. Pennypacker Memorial Park yesterday without bringing anyone with me. So what?

But it made me think about what Alfie said.

Maybe I *am* running out of fwends. I mean *friends*.

Everyone in my class seems to like me just fine, except for Jared Matthews, sometimes. But he takes turns being grouchy with everyone. And Stanley Washington is kind of like Jared's personal assistant, the way Fiona McNulty is Cynthia Harbison's personal assistant, so sometimes he stays away from me, too.

Cynthia says that movie stars have personal assistants, so why not her?

It's her latest thing.

Cynthia is basically the girl version of Jared in our class, only worse. She thinks faster than Jared, and she speaks up quicker.

I will take a new look at all the guys in my class before school starts tomorrow morning. It would be great to make at least one spare friend by this Friday, because that's when Alfie's show is going to be. My new friend and I can sit through that, then we will all go out for pizza or ice cream, so that will be fun. And then we can have a sleepover, which will be the most fun of all.

I already know Corey can't do it, because he has swim practice every Saturday morning. Early, like at six-thirty.

There are only ten boys in Ms. Sanchez's third grade class, and there are fifteen girls That means the girls are winning—in population, anyway. But it also means there are five other guys in my class—besides Corey, Kevin, Stanley, and Jared— for me to be friends with. Maybe.

The five extra boys are: Major Donaldson, Marco Adair, Nate Marshall, Jason Leffer, and Diego Romero.

Those are my possibilities.

Major mostly hangs out with Marco. In fact, Ms. Sanchez sometimes calls them "M and M" for short. When she calls on Marco in class, though, she usually calls him Mr. Adair, because when she accidentally calls out, "Marco," someone always says, "*Polo!*"

And everybody laughs.

Third-graders need easy stuff like that to laugh about, in my opinion. Our school days are long, and we get desperate for entertainment.

There are lots of reasons to like Marco Adair. He's always fair with the kickballs, and with choosing sides when we play games at recess. Also, he can make funny armpit noises better than any other boy in our class. Only on the playground, of course. Ms. Sanchez is not the type of lady who would think it's funny when you make your armpit go **FLIRRRRPPT.**

Major Donaldson is cool, too. In fact, my dad claims that Major has the best name in the world, because the word "major" means so many different things.

1. Major can mean *important*, like when someone says, "This is really major."
2. It also has something to do with music. I forget what.

3. And in college, Dad says that your major is
   the main thing you study. For example, my
   dad's major was geology. My mom's major was
   comparative literature, whatever that means.
   I don't know yet what my major in college will be.
   Maybe the History of Video Games?
4. But best of all, a major is a very important officer
   in the armed services, like the army or the
   marines.

My dad teases, threatening to salute whenever he sees Major Donaldson. That's the kind of sense of humor he has.

The only problem is, Marco and Major are so tight that it might be hard to squeeze my way into being their friend. There might not be enough room. They've known each other since kindergarten, and they're not sick of each other yet.

Nate Marshall is another friend possibility, though. He doesn't hang with anyone special. His red hair sticks up in front, like he's got a little rooster crest there. But on him it looks good—like an exclamation point.

The most unusual thing about Nate—that I

know of, anyway—is how much he knows about cars. Well, about vehicles in general. They are his obsession. What he *really* loves is to explain something like spark plugs, for example. He goes on and on until you can either prove you understand what he's saying, which I hate, or until the school buzzer sounds. Whatever comes first.

I'll keep Nate in reserve. He's not perfect, but I could probably fix that.

Jason Leffer might be a better friend possibility. His name should be Jason *Laugh-er*, because he turned into the class funny guy last fall. And he's not just funny with words, even though he does tell a pretty good knock-knock joke. But he also owns fake dog-doo and rubber barf, useful prank stuff like that. And he sneaked a whoopee cushion into school one day a couple of weeks ago.

In case you didn't know, a whoopee cushion is sort of a balloon pancake that you blow air into, and then it makes a really gross noise when your joke victim sits on it. Marco Adair the armpit noise king thinks it's hysterical, of course.

But even Jason doesn't dare try out the whoopee cushion on beautiful Ms. Sanchez.

Ms. Sanchez and whoopee cushions do not go together. Also, our class would never forgive Jason if she sat down at her desk one day in a pretty dress and made that noise.

Nobody wants her to get embarrassed so close to her getting married. The girls all say that her head is filled with wedding stuff—not to mention what the man who is going to be Ms. Sanchez's husband would say or do if someone insulted her.

His name is Mr. Timberlake, but he's not the *famous* Mr. Timberlake. Ms. Sanchez's Mr. Timberlake runs a sporting goods store full of bats, nets, balls, surfboards, and climbing gear. And he looks like he knows how to play every single sport, surf each giant wave, and climb every mountain or climbing wall better than anyone. So none of us guys wants to make him anything even *close* to mad.

The truth is, lots of kids—like me, for instance— secretly wish Ms. Sanchez would just stay the same as always, *forever*, without having a new husband hanging around at open houses and assemblies. She acts different when he's here.

And she's got enough to think about with us kids, hasn't she?

Jason is kind of a chunky guy, but it's mostly muscle, he says. And I believe him. He has buzz-cut hair, like the fur of this hedgehog I saw once in a nature book. And his ears stick out a little, but in a good way. You definitely know they're there.

I think I could turn Jason into a pretty cool friend, especially if I can get him to stop making jokes and pulling pranks all the time. Stuff like that is funny, and I love funny. But it can wear a person out after a while.

Also, I like the chance to be funny, too.

My last friend possibility is Diego Romero. My mom says that *his* name sounds like it belongs to a movie star. And I can tell that a couple of girls in our class kind of like him, even though Diego is a quiet guy. He likes to read. He even reads instructions! And sometimes he brings these really thick books to school to share with Ms. Sanchez.

But he's not a kiss-up, he's cool. And I think I could loosen him up.

Okay. Now that I think about it, maybe none of

these five guys is *perfect*, but like I said about Nate, I can fix that. All I have to do is to hang out with them more, get to know them better. Starting tomorrow morning.

And then I can choose which kid I want to be my spare friend.

Who will it be? Major, Marco, Nate, Jason, or Diego?

Maybe the winner can even become *my* personal assistant some day! I know Corey's way too busy winning swim meets and polishing his medals to take on that role, even if he would. But having a personal assistant does sound pretty cool.

Now, all I need is to figure out who the lucky kid will be.

It would be great to have a new friend by Friday, the day of Alfie's show. But my long-term goal is to have one by the end of this month.

January.

Then I'll have a happy new year for sure!

✳ **3** ✳

SECRET PLAN

"Hurry up, EllRay," Mom says as I shovel a last spoonful of cereal into my mouth. The spoon is heaped so high that the milk in it trickles down my wrist. It makes my sleeve feel wet and sticky.

What's the big deal about making me take a shower and then put on clean clothes every morning, when messy stuff like trickling cereal milk happens before I'm even out the door?

Give it up, Mom! It's hopeless.

"Don't forget your lunch," my mother reminds me.

Like I *would*. Food is just about my favorite thing. Also playing, and TV. "Where's Alfie?" I ask, trying to turn the mom-spotlight away from me for a second.

"She's upstairs, changing her barrettes," Mom says, shaking her head. My mom is tall, thin, and pretty, and her skin is the color of the best caramel you ever saw. She likes to wear headbands, but not the scary plastic kind with teeth that Cynthia Harbison wears to school. Cynthia's headbands look like they're mad at her head. "Alfie forgot that she already wore the barrettes she put on this morning," Mom tries to explain. "Just last Thursday. It was a narrow escape," she adds, laughing.

Alfie is turning into a fashion diva, Mom says. Whatever a diva is.

I think it means spoiled.

"She better not make me late for school," I say.

See, Dad has already left, because he has an hour-long drive to San Diego. Like I already said, he teaches geology at a college there. So Mom has to drive both Alfie and me to school every day. Alfie gets dropped off first each morning, and sometimes it takes her a long time to leave the car.

Here is an example of how hard it can be to get Alfie to leave Mom's Toyota. One morning when Alfie was about to get out of the car at school, she discovered that she had put on shoes from two different pairs of sneakers, one pink and one blue. That was a *major* meltdown. Alfie cried so hard that she yakked out the car window, and then she and Mom had to go home and lie down after they dropped me off at Oak Glen and Mom hosed off the car.

I'm glad I missed that part of the morning.

Another time, Mom caught Alfie trying to sneak a new doll into school. That's against the law at Kreative Learning and Daycare—which has a sign outside that my dad just loves, for some reason. The sign reads, *Featuring Spanish, Computer Skills, and Potty Training.* Dad sometimes makes a joke about how hard it would be to teach all three things at once.

I guess that's how teachers think. Even college teachers.

But like I said, Alfie sometimes refuses to leave Mom's car, which is why I'm worried about being late on this very important Monday.

Day one of my secret plan.

The day when I figure out which new friend to choose.

"EllWay, *c'mon*," Alfie is saying, hands on her hips as she stares at me from the kitchen doorway. "Wake up!"

"I'm awake," I tell her. "Anyway, Mom and I were waiting for *you*, slow-poke."

"Mom's already in the car," Alfie informs me. "And me and my cute barrettes don't wanna be late."

"Me neither," I say, locking the kitchen door behind me on my way out.

Not today, of all days, I add to myself.

4

LIKE A SPY

Oak Glen Primary School goes from kindergarten through sixth grade, which puts our third grade class right in the middle, if you count kindergarten. And us third grade kids are in the middle sizewise, too, except for me. I am the shortest kid—boy or girl—in Ms. Sanchez's class, and I have been all semester. I keep hoping that someone even shorter will transfer in, like a leprechaun maybe, but no such luck.

Dad tells me I'll start growing taller pretty soon, but when?

If the weather is nice, which it almost always is in Oak Glen, we play outside near the picnic tables before school starts. Well, the boys play, and the girls in our class mostly just hang, talk or whisper, and make fun of us boys. My opinion is that the girls don't want to mess up their clothes first thing in the morning. Excuse me, their *outfits*.

They save their running around for later in the day.

I walk toward the picnic tables as if I am seeing the guys in my class for the first time. I feel like a spy.

"Hey, EllRay!" my friend Corey calls out, waving at me.

Corey has blond hair and freckles, and he usually smells like chlorine. He works out before school at a swimming pool in an Oak Glen gym, that's why. And then, after school, he works out at an aquatics center in a bigger town nearby.

"Aquatics" means doing stuff in the water.

An aquatics center has more than one pool, Corey says. Also, they're longer and more official looking. And nobody has fun there, the way Corey tells it.

But he's having fun now, at least. Corey is playing with a wooden paddleboard, his latest obsession. He must have sneaked it into school in his backpack. This doesn't break any *big* rule, except for the one that says you can't bring toys to school.

And Cynthia and Fiona say that the paddle part of the toy could be used as a weapon. They keep threatening to tell on him.

But Cynthia's toothy *headband* could be used as a weapon.

So could a book, if it was thick enough!

Corey says that paddleboarding is a sport—this kind of paddleboarding, with a red rubber ball attached to a small paddle by a piece of elastic string,

not the kind you do standing on a board in the ocean. And grownups are always trying to get us kids to do more sports, aren't they?

They have meetings about it all the time. With *cake*.

Also, Corey never plays with his paddleboard in class.

I'm not saying he's *right* to sneak it into school. I'm just reporting the facts.

Another fact is that until he gets caught and the paddleboard gets taken away from him, Corey is likely to keep bringing it to Oak Glen. "Watch this," he tells me, bouncing the ball off the board about ten times in a row.

BAM, BAM, BAM, BAM, BAM, BAM, BAM, BAM, BAM, BAM.

"Don't you dare hit me with that thing, Corey Robinson, or I'm telling," Cynthia calls out from one of the girls' picnic tables, right on schedule. She is about ten feet away from Corey, who, of course, ignores her.

I sneak a spy-like peek over at Marco and Major, who are playing on the beat-up grass. They are huddled over these little plastic knights Marco collects—and sneaks into school.

We don't mean to be bad. We are just trying to have some extra fun.

I think Marco would live in the olden days if he could, and Major would be right there with him!

Me, I'm more of a modern day kind of kid. I like cell phones and tablets, and the more apps stuffed into everything the better. Most of all, I like video games. My current favorite one is *Die, Creature, Die.* I got it for Christmas. It's handheld but still cool.

They didn't have *that* in the olden days, Marco.

I shift my sneaky spy gaze over to Nate Marshall. His red rooster crest looks extra perky today. He is explaining something to Kevin, who looks confused. Kevin is trying to sneak away. "See?" Nate is saying, keeping up with him, like they have magnets in their legs. "Don't you get it? The cylinder head *delivers* the spark."

"Sort of. I think I get it," Kevin says, looking around in a *"Save me!"* kind of way. I think Kevin is afraid there's going to be a quiz, and school hasn't even started yet!

Hmm, I think. Turning Nate into a spare friend might be too much work. Especially now, when I need fast results.

Meanwhile, Jason Leffer is laughing with Jared and Stanley on the other side of one of the boys' picnic tables. I think he's pretending he just pulled a giant booger out of his nose, only it's really a raisin from his lunch sack.

Excuse me for saying "booger." I am just reporting the facts.

"He's gonna eat it," Fiona shrieks from one of the girls' picnic tables.

They don't officially have "girls' tables" or "boys' tables" at Oak Glen Primary School, by the way. I think doing that is against the law. It just works out that way, about girls' tables and boys' tables, once you get past first or second grade.

I forget. That was a long time ago.

The point is, Jason is *fun*.

But Diego Romero can be fun, too, I remind myself. Right now, Diego is leaning against a tree, reading a car magazine. I don't know much about cars, but the magazine looks pretty cool. And once Diego is my friend, I can sort of scooch him over to stuff that doesn't involve reading. Things *I* like to do.

So, Diego and Jason it is, I decide. If I play this right, I'll have *two* spare friends!

A spare, and a spare-spare.

Alfie will be so impressed. She'll feel good about coming to Oak Glen Primary School next year.

"Hey," I say, scuffing my way over to Diego's tree. "Cars, huh?"

Brilliant, EllRay.

"Yeah," Diego says, marking his place with a finger and looking up at me with a friendly smile.

Hey. An accidental good start!

"What kind of car do you want to have when you turn sixteen?" Diego asks me, really curious.

Not my mom's old one, that's for sure, is all I can think. Because after all, turning sixteen is eight years away. And that's a whole other lifetime, since I'm only eight years old *now*.

But luckily, the warning buzzer sounds before I have to answer Diego. "Later, dude," I say, trying to match his earlier smile without being too weird. But Diego's not even looking at me. He's too busy getting his stuff together.

"Dude," Corey calls out, winding the elastic string loosely around his paddleboard handle and jamming it into his backpack. "Who you growlin' at?"

"Nobody," I say, trying to erase my goofy smile as we all head toward class.

Just a normal Monday morning, I tell myself. But things are looking up!

I've made my choice. My *choices*, I mean.

Now, all I need is to find a way to get Diego's and Jason's attention so they'll *want* to be my friends.

✳ 5 ✳

ELLRAY JAKES THE
RECESS KING!

"You're awfully quiet over there, buddy," Dad says at dinner.

Turkey meatloaf, a huge blob of ketchup, carrot coins, and my mom's special potatoes.

"I'm good," I tell him.

"EllWay's just thinking," Alfie explains.

She's actually right. I have been trying to figure out the best way to make Jason and Diego want to be my friends. I mean, we're already *friends*, I guess, since we have been in the same class since September, and we have never had a fight.

But I want them to be *real* friends.

Friends I can hang with after school, on weekends, and even during the summer.

Friends like Corey is, when he's not busy swimming, or like Kevin is some of the time.

"Hold on a second, EllRay," Dad says, his always-solemn face creasing into an even more serious expression. "Is everything okay at school?"

His fork has stopped halfway to his mouth.

"Now, Warren," my mom says, probably hoping to calm him down.

Okay. Here's what is going on.

1. My mom and dad moved us to Oak Glen from San Diego when I was in kindergarten, even though the move meant that Dad would have a much longer drive to work. All the way down to San Diego—and back.

2. But almost the minute we got to Oak Glen, I think my dad was bothered that there weren't more brown faces around town.

3. What worried him even more was the idea that kids my class might pick on me because my skin *is* brown. And when Alfie came along, *whoa*.

4. So far, there hasn't been any trouble like that. There are plenty of *real* reasons for kids to get irked with me, and the other way around! Me with

them, I mean. And the same with Alfie, for that matter. *Normal* reasons.

5. But Dad's worries still stick in his head—like a splinter, I guess. You know how, when you have a splinter in your hand, and you can't get it out, the thought of it always fills your brain? Even though the splinter is only in one little part of your body?

   Like that.

   Like the way I feel about being short.

"I'm only asking, Louise," Dad tells my mom, putting down his fork. "It's a perfectly reasonable question."

Notice how my mom and dad get to have regular names, by the way? Louise and Warren? But Alfie and I have names we have to *explain*.

Like I said, parents should not do that to their kids. In my opinion.

"Don't worry, Dad. Everything is fine at school," I say. "I just feel kind of quiet tonight, but in a *good* way. Like Alfie said, I'm thinking."

"Anyway, *I'm* the chatterbox around here," Alfie says, sounding proud.

As if we needed telling!

"And you'll never guess where Suzette Monahan thinks baby kitties come from," my little sister adds. She leans forward, her brown eyes wide.

"Oh, heaven help us," Mom says. "Here we go."

And—I actually stop trying to figure out how to con Jason and Diego into being my friends for a minute. What Alfie says next will either be completely rando, like our teenage babysitter says, or it'll be really good.

Dad looks worried again. "I'm not sure that telling us where kittens come from is the best subject for the dinner table, Alfleta," he says.

Alfleta. *"Beautiful elf,"* in a language only my mom knows anymore.

See what I mean?

"Why?" Alfie asks, her golden face starting to crumple. "You don't like *flowers*? Because that's where Suzette found a whole *bunch* of kitties, she said. In their garden. And she'll sell us one for only a hundred dollars."

And Mom, Dad, and I all start to laugh—which, of course, only makes things worse with Alfie.

But that's okay, because she gets over things fast.

I guess she doesn't have any brain splinters yet.

Later, in bed, I stare at my ceiling in the dark. I am trying to figure out my friend problem in a logical way. That's what Dad is always telling me to do. "Be logical."

He's a scientist, remember.

Jason Leffer is already the funny kid in our class, I remind myself. So I can't win him over with pranks and jokes. Diego, either.

And I can't *bribe* them into being my friends. I don't have enough money! I only have enough saved up to bribe maybe half a person for five minutes, tops.

My dad says I'm one of life's big spenders, that's the thing.

Besides, Mom and Dad would never let me get away with something as bad as bribery.

But there's another thing I'm good at beside

spending money, and that's having fun. I can really get into it.

And when does a kid have the most fun at school?

During recess.

So if I can figure out a way to be the most fun kid in the world at recess, if I can turn into the kid with the best ideas of stuff to do, then Jason and Diego are sure to want to be my new spare friends!

I can fix what's wrong with them after that, I tell myself—like Jason cracking jokes all the time, and Diego thinking there's nothing better to do than read.

They'll *thank* me someday.

But first, I have to become EllRay Jakes, the recess king!

Genius.

✳ 6 ✳

COMPUTER TIME

"Can I use the computer after dinner?" I ask Dad. It is Tuesday, the day after I got my bright idea.

I don't tell my dad that I need to do some research. If I tell him that, he will peek over my shoulder and make suggestions the whole time. Dad *loves* research.

But this is my thing.

"I think you mean *may* you use the computer after dinner," Dad says. His look shows that he has covered this subject a number of times before.

Okay, about a zillion.

"Because yes, you *can* use the computer," he continues. "You are physically able to use it, of course. But *may* you use it? That involves getting permission, and permission is a whole different matter. Is your homework done?"

"Yes," I say, remembering at the last second not to say, *"Yup."*

Because then there would be a whole different lecture.

Dad says it's the little things in life that count. But he turns everything into something big.

"I finished my homework before dinner," I tell him. And even *I* sound amazed. On a normal night, I can gripe so long about my homework that it doesn't get done until minutes before bedtime.

Not tonight, though!

"That's my boy," Dad says, looking pleased. "And yes, you *may* have some computer time. I'll keep you company while your mom tackles Alfie's bath."

Our big computer is in the family room, and Alfie and I have to ask permission to use it. I guess the idea is that Mom and Dad want to keep track of what we're doing on the computer. That's probably not such a bad idea, or Alfie might start buying stuff online. Barbie mansions, buckets of candy, the cutest outfits in the world, you name it. At the very least, she would buy more plastic horses, a glittery stable, and a golden corral big enough to go around our entire house, if they make such a thing.

Luckily, she doesn't know how to buy things on-line. *Yet.*

Neither do I.

But my plan tonight is to research a bunch of amazing things to do at recess. Then I can look like I'm thinking up brilliant ideas—***WHAM!*** just like that!—while us guys are hanging out, doing the usual boring recess stuff. They'll be saying, *"Whaddya wanna do?"* And, *"I dunno. What do you want to do?"* over and over again.

It's kind of our thing.

And then I, EllRay Jakes the recess king, will come up with something great.

Who wouldn't want to be friends with a new-idea-guy like that? I mean, like me?

The new and *improved* me.

I drag the big chair in toward the desk and make a list of things to look up. You have to be careful on the Internet, or you can jump to some really weird stuff by accident. And then you will never be allowed to use the computer again until you are an old man—at least not at *my* house.

But here is my list of things to look up:

1. Playground games.

2. Third grade recess.

3. Ideas for recess games.

You have to give the computer lots of hints and choices to get your research started.

Mom and Dad would be okay with me looking up those three things.

As usual, *boom*, just like that, some of the sites try to sell me something: a pair of shiny high heeled

shoes, vitamins, life insurance. I don't even know what life insurance is, but it sounds like a tough guy high school threat, like, "You better do what I say—*or else.*"

They don't know I'm just a kid with no money.

Better luck next time, ads.

But there are some sites with pretty good ideas, I see, scrolling down. A few of them even have videos that some faraway primary schools made. They show sample kids playing sample games. The kids look a little embarrassed, knowing they're being filmed, but the games aren't bad.

I pull my notebook closer so I can write stuff down. But first, in my brain, I cross off every online idea that starts with *equipment*, even simple equipment such as tarps, tires, or those foam noodles kids play with in swimming pools. We're not supposed to bring stuff like that to school. It might mess up our playground's special design, I guess.

That design is basically an empty square, except for the grassy hill where our picnic tables sit. There is a paved area with a couple of overhead ladders, some creaky swings, and a slide. A first grader hurled all over the top step of the slide ladder last week, so now no one wants to use it.

It's been scrubbed clean, but no takers.

Oh, and there's a locked storage shed in the corner of our playground. It's full of deflated kickballs and grimy hula hoops, even though it's only January. There are five months to go before school is over for the year.

Too bad for us, I guess.

I cross off all the girl activities, too.

I decide to write down ten things in my notebook, then choose my cool recess ideas from those. What I really want is to find special activities that Jason Leffer and Diego Romero will want to do!

Funny stuff for Jason, and I'm-not-sure-what-kind-of-stuff for Diego.

Nothing to do with reading during recess, that's for sure.

After I rope Jason and Diego in with how much fun I am, I can teach them the kinds of things *I* like to do, like playing Sky High Foursquare or Shadow Tag. Running-around stuff like that.

Then I'll have a friend, *Corey*, a half-friend, *Kevin*, a spare friend, *Jason*, and a spare-spare friend, *Diego*.

I will be rich. Rich in friends!

"You about done here, buddy?" Dad asks over my shoulder. "Did you find what you were looking for? Because you need some time for your eyes to unwind after using the computer, you know. And your mom wants to read to you."

I nod, trying not to think of my eyes unwinding, which is just gross. Dad says stuff in a complicated way sometimes, probably because he is so smart. But I kind of know what he means. A person's eyes do get jumpy, staring at the computer screen. But computers are cool! You can look up anything.

1. I can look up my own dad on the Internet.
2. I can spy on any place in the world in one second flat.
3. I can even scare myself, looking at pictures of leopard sharks or hungry polar bears who might be looking for an EllRay sandwich.

Mom reading to me will be the perfect medicine for my jumpy eyes, even though the book she's reading me is very exciting. It is *The Sword in the Stone*, by T. H. White. I guess the first part of his name is a secret. That's why he uses his initials.

The book is a lot different from the old cartoon movie version Alfie has. In the book, the wizard Merlyn turns Wart—who grows up to become King Arthur, Mom says—into lots of different animals, and Wart learns something important from each one. For example, in the chapter we are reading now, Merlyn turns Wart into a goose. Wart learns that geese don't fight each other. They stick together, fly together, and protect each other. They only fight when they are attacked by outsiders.

Unlike some of the other animals, like ants—who *love* to fight.

"Then shut her down and go brush your teeth," Dad says, knuckle-rubbing my hair—which only he is allowed to do. It's his version of a hug.

"Her." Our family room computer is a girl, I guess. That's strange. Well, girls *are* pretty smart.

"Okay, Dad," I say, ducking my head and grabbing my notebook. "Good night."

"Night, son," my dad says, and he gives my chicken-bone shoulder a dadly squeeze.

He's pretty cool, my dad!

✳ 7 ✳

A VERY GOOD IDEA

"I forgot to ask you something," I say to Mom the next morning, right before we leave for school.

I timed it this way.

"What is it?" Mom asks, sounding busy as she finishes up my lunch—which I plan to eat before the first buzzer rings.

"I need to bring something to school," I tell her. "From the pointy closet. Can I go get it?"

We have this weird closet under the stairs. You can't hang coats in it because the ceiling slopes, so Mom decided it was the perfect place to keep the extra stuff we get at that huge store up the freeway. The store where you have to buy twenty boxes of tissues at a time, or huge jars of pickles. *That* place.

"What do you need?" Mom asks, washing her hands at the sink and then looking around for Alfie.

"TP," I whisper.

"Excuse me? What did you say?" my mom asks, turning to face me.

Great. I have her full attention, and I was hoping to slip this one past her.

"TP," I repeat, shrugging. "That's short for toilet paper, Mom."

"I know what it's short for," Mom says, her eyes wide. "Are you telling me that you're supposed to bring your own toilet paper to school these days? Things are *that bad*?"

"We don't *have* to bring it," I say, sliding my eyes away from hers as I cross my fingers behind my back.

No, I haven't told a lie yet. But I'm getting kind of close.

It's true that I don't *like* the TP at Oak Glen Primary School. It isn't like regular TP at all. It's not even rolled up. School TP is more like little squares of tissue paper stuffed into a metal box. But it's okay. At least it's paper. It's not like we have to use leaves or something.

"Hmm," Mom says, thinking.

The truth is, I need that roll of TP—or I *want*

it—for my plan to coax Jason Leffer into being my spare friend. It'll be a start, anyway.

"We're late," Alfie shouts, skipping into the kitchen in a pink and purple blur. "And I get to be the magic kitty this morning! So let's *go!*"

Mom is still staring at me. It's like she's counting up all the things that are wrong with Oak Glen Primary School.

"Listen, Mom," I say. "Never mind. I—"

"EllRay, for heaven's sake. Go ahead and take a roll of toilet paper," she says, shaking her head as she gathers up our things. "Of *course* you can bring your own TP to school if you need to. Grab a roll from the open package, and stash it in your backpack, if there's room."

"*What?*" Alfie asks, as if she can't believe what she just heard.

"It's a long story," I tell her.

"It better be a quick one, EllWay," she says, looking half curious, half grossed-out, and half crazy-impatient to leave.

Wait. That's one too many halves.

But in less than ten seconds, I zip into the hall, open the closet door, grab a roll of TP from the tower of supplies jammed inside, and cram the roll into my backpack.

Man, I hope it doesn't fall out at an embarrassing time.

1. That roll of TP could tumble out of my backpack on the front steps of the school, where Principal James greets each of us by name in the morning. It could bounce down the cement steps, *bump, bump, bump.* I would never live it down.

2. Or the roll of TP might fall out of my backpack as I walk down the hall toward class. I would leave a long trail of paper behind me.

   Not. Gonna. Happen.

3. Or the roll of TP could topple out of my backpack and onto the floor in our cubby closet in front of *all the girls*, when I'm putting my stuff away. "Lose something?" Cynthia would ask, waving the roll of TP in the air for all to see.

There are a lot of disaster possibilities when you bring a roll of toilet paper to school.

This better be worth it.

"Paper and pencils out, girls and boys, boys and girls," Ms. Sanchez tells us right after she takes attendance. She likes to treat us equally. "We're having a quiz on the spelling words from the last two weeks," she says. "Surprise!"

Ms. Sanchez is usually a very nice lady. But saying *"Surprise!"* in such a situation is just mean, in my opinion. She always tells us that she wants us to know how to spell words *forever,* though, and not just for the week of the quiz. Ms. Sanchez says she does not want our motto to be, *"In one ear and out the other."*

I think that means she wants the words to stay in our brains for a long time. Long enough for us to be able to use them again in an emergency, for example. Although in my opinion, *short* words are probably best when it comes to emergencies.

Words like, *"Fire!"* and *"Help!"* and *"Giant snakes!"*

Our low chorus of grumbles is muffled by the **CLANK** of our three-ring binders and the

R-R-R-RIP! of notebook paper being wrestled from them.

If we could make any more noise, we would.

"*Stairs*," Ms. Sanchez begins. "As in the stairs that you climb. And use each of your words in a sentence, please."

I'm a pretty good speller most of the time. "S-T-A-I-R-S," I print. "*We walk down the stairs to the playground.*"

"*Sometimes*," Ms. Sanchez says, moving on to the second word.

"S-O-M-T-I-M-E-S," I write, smiling as I think about the recess to come. Awesome! "*Somtimes I get a very good idea.*"

I'm not sure yet how to spell "excellent," or I'd say "*an excellent idea.*"

"*Prepared*," Ms. Sanchez says, perching on the edge of her desk and admiring the toe of one of her shoes. There's a bow on it.

"P-R-E-P-A-R-E-D," I print, my pointer finger already creased from the pencil. "*I am prepared to make a new friend.*"

And on and on our teacher goes.

This is going to be the longest morning ever. E-V-E-R.

But it'll be worth the wait, I tell myself, half hiding a secret smile.

Recess is gonna be *so much fun.*

✳ 8 ✳

THE CURSE OF
THE MUMMY ZOMBIE

"You look weird," Emma McGraw says as we push our way out the classroom door and into the hall, because—it's finally recess! "Do you have a tummy ache?" she asks.

All the other guys are already out on the playground. I'm losing recess time.

"I'm fine," I tell her. I am just trying to hide the roll of toilet paper under my jacket. "And P.S., Emma," I say. "You shouldn't tell people they look weird."

"But you do look weird," Annie Pat Masterson says. She is defending Emma, her best friend. "No offense," she adds.

"I don't think you can say '*you look weird*' and '*no offense*' at the same time," Kry Rodriguez says as we make our way down the crowded hall.

Me and *three girls*.

Emma, Annie Pat, and Kry are the best girls in our class, though. They don't whisper or giggle behind their hands when a boy messes up, or act like they're so great, the way Cynthia and Fiona sometimes do.

But this was not the way I wanted this special morning recess to start.

"Bye-ya," I tell Emma, Annie Pat, and Kry, and *zoom!* off I go, heading for the door like a football player racing toward the end zone.

Okay, like a *small* football player—holding a roll of TP instead of a ball.

"No running in the halls," I hear a grownup yell behind me, but I'm already gone.

Jason Leffer, here I come!

"Look who's finally here," Stanley calls as I come trotting up, still hiding the TP under my jacket.

"C'mon, EllRay. We're about to play Bubblegum

Foursquare," my sometimes-friend Kevin says. He bounces the dark red ball a couple of times to tempt me.

Bubblegum Foursquare is really fun. In the Oak Glen Primary School version, the fourth person to hit the ball has to stay frozen to that spot for the rest of the game—like they're stuck there with gum.

But I have other plans. "Later, dog," I say, looking for Jason.

He's over at the boys' picnic table with Corey, Diego, and Major. They're stuffing their faces, of course. "Hey," I say, walking over to the table. "Have you guys ever played Mummy Zombie?"

"Never heard of it," Corey says through his turkey-cheese roll-up.

Corey's big into protein. Or his mom is, anyway.

"And I've never *read* of it," Diego says.

"Then it doesn't exist," Jason announces, laughing. "EllRay's just making stuff up—probably because he already ate all his food."

"I'll share," Corey offers, holding out his drooping snack.

"No, thanks. I'm good," I say, looking around for the playground monitor. It's Mr. Havens today, but he's way across the playground. He's huge and he teaches second grade. I guess he's subbing for the real monitor.

I take out the roll of TP from under my jacket. "Ta-da!" I say, holding it up.

"Dude," Jason says, slapping his forehead like he cannot believe his eyes. "You can't use that stuff out here. You gotta go *inside*, to the room that says *Boys* on the door. Right, guys?" he asks, already cracking up at his own joke.

"No. Listen, Jase," I say, pulling the end of the paper free. "I saw this on the Internet. The 'mummy' part, anyway. I made up the rest. But see, I'm gonna wrap this TP all around you, and turn you into a mummy *zombie*, okay? And then whoever you tag *also* has to be a zombie. Except only you get to be the *king* mummy zombie," I add, trying to make it sound extra special.

Jason's eyes light up, and his buzz-cut hair seems to sent out sparks. "Do it," he says, holding out his arms. "Wrap me up quick, dude. I'm in!"

"I need some help," I say to the guys sitting at the picnic table. Corey, Diego, and Major have stopped chewing, I see.

This is perfect! I have made Jason Leffer the star of morning recess, which is probably a dream come true for him.

Of course he will want to be my new spare friend!

"C'mon, you guys," I say. And in two seconds, Corey, Diego, and Major are helping me wrap the toilet paper all over Jason: around his middle a few times, then up around one arm, then across to the other arm. And then we start in on his fuzzy mummy zombie head.

"RAW-R-R-R-R!" Jason bellows, getting into it.

By now, of course, we have a pretty big audience.

"The buzzer's gonna sound," Corey warns, and Jason takes off into the crowd.

"RAW—R—R—R—R!" he howls again, staggering stiff-legged toward the kids that surround us. He reaches out his arms. Flaps of TP trail behind him like—well, like flaps of TP. A couple of pieces of toilet paper float free.

"It's the curse of the mummy zombie," Major yells, explaining it to the running kids. "And if he tags you, you have to be a zombie too! Like, *forever*," he adds, waving his own arms in the air.

Hey. I didn't say *forever*. My own game is getting away from me!

But, **"EEE–E–E–E–E!"** everyone shouts, scattering wide. The girls are laughing and screaming at the same time.

"What's a zombie?" a little boy asks. He's a first-grader, I think. What's he doing over here with us big kids? Is he lost or something?

"Zombie—gonna—get—you," Jason yells, heading first for the bunch of third grade girls, and then lurching back toward the little boy. "Zombie gonna *eat* you."

"WAH-H-H-H-H," the kid cries. His fists are up against his mouth. He is frozen where he stands.

This kid will be really good at Bubblegum Four-square some day, I can't help but think. Only that's not what we're playing right now.

This is out of control.

And not in a good way.

"Don't eat me," the little guy begs, trying to hide his head with the front of his red zippered sweatshirt. He crumples onto the grass, surrendering.

"It's only pretend, kid," I yell as a couple more toilet paper squares flutter to the ground.

TWE–E–E–E–T!

A whistle blows about two inches from my ear.

It's Mr. Havens, the gigantic playground monitor. And boy, does he look mad!

"Exactly *what* is supposed to be happening here?" he shouts, his big hands on his hips.

And nobody moves, not even the little boy on the grass.

It's like Bubblegum *Recess*, we're all holding so still.

✳ 9 ✳
EPIC FAIL

"This is all your fault, Mr. Mummy," Cynthia whispers to Jason—the mummy zombie king—as we file back into Ms. Sanchez's classroom. It's like we are cartoon bad guys marching off to jail in black-and-white striped uniforms. Ms. Sanchez is still in the hall talking to Mr. Havens.

I guess this was not his lucky day to substitute.

Join the crowd, Mr. Havens.

Jason shoots me a dirty look, but he doesn't say anything. There are a couple of squares of TP still hanging from the back pocket of his jeans, but I pretend I don't see them.

"Yeah, *Mr. Mummy*," Fiona echoes, glaring at Jason. "You made that little boy cry."

"Everyone was having fun until that happened," loyal Corey points out, giving me a secret nudge of support.

"I didn't see how it started," Annie Pat complains. "Where did all that toilet paper come from?"

"It was probably Jared's bright idea," Cynthia announces, scowling.

All the boys in our class, even Jared, make a point of not looking at Cynthia—or at me. But they *know* where that roll of toilet paper came from.

I guess us guys are gonna stick together on this one. We're like the loyal geese in *The Sword in the Stone.* For now, anyway.

In terms of making a new spare friend, though, this has to go down as an epic fail. Jason Leffer looks like he'll never laugh again.

Good one, EllRay. So much for inviting Jason over Friday—to see Alfie's goofy play, and then maybe have pizza or ice cream, and some sleepover fun.

Ms. Sanchez comes gliding back into the classroom like the ice queen in one of Alfie's cartoon movies. "Well," she begins, sitting down. "Imagine my surprise." She lays her hands flat on top of the desk, which is kind of scary for some reason.

"Us *girls* didn't do anything," Cynthia says, talking and raising her hand at the same time.

"Quiet, please, Miss Harbison," Ms. Sanchez says, not even looking at Cynthia.

Uh-oh. She calls us "Miss" and Mister" when she's really angry.

"We have some things to sort out," Ms. Sanchez says in a solemn voice. "Now, we *were* going to do some math word problems before lunch," she continues.

Math word problems are usually pretty fun, unless your name is Corey Robinson. Corey can compete in a swim race in front of one-hundred people, and win, but math makes him panic.

Here is an example of a math word problem, in case you didn't know:

There are twenty-five (25) students in Ms. Sanchez's third grade class. Ten (10) of them are boys. One (1) boy hates math word problems. How many boys in Ms. Sanchez's class don't hate math word problems?

"And then," Ms. Sanchez continues, "as a reward for working so hard on your math, I was going to read aloud to you. It was a really funny book, too. But I guess we won't have time for that, now," she says, shaking her head.

Corey's hand inches up. "What do we have to do instead?" he asks in a nervous voice after Ms. Sanchez calls on him.

He's probably worried it'll be something even *worse* than math word problems.

Like taking out our own tonsils, maybe.

"I'm so glad you asked, Mr. Robinson," Ms. Sanchez says. "First, you will all write notes of apology to Iggy Brown."

"Who's Iggy Brown?" Emma asks, not even raising her hand first. She sounds one-hundred percent (100%) confused.

"Iggy Brown is the little first-grade boy who got knocked down by a bunch of stampeding third-graders at morning recess," Ms. Sanchez says, her voice cool.

"Nobody knocked him down," Jason mumbles. "He *collapsed.*"

"Did you say something, Mr. Leffer?" Ms. Sanchez asks.

"Nuh-uh," he says, shaking his head.

"Good," Ms. Sanchez says. "Because poor little Iggy was really scared. His mama is having to leave work to bring him a change of clothes, so he can finish out the day."

"It wasn't *that* dirty on the grass," Marco says, his voice low—but not low enough.

"Do you have something to contribute, Mr. Adair?" Ms. Sanchez asks.

"Nope," Marco says, sounding hopeless.

"Me neither," Major chimes in.

He's the other M in "M and M," remember?

"Iggy wet his pants because of the mummy," Fiona loud-whispers. "I saw. It was sad. Poor little guy."

"Poor little guy," the other girls echo.

And I kind of agree with them. Because what if it had been my little sister Alfie, and not Iggy, who wandered over to the wrong area of the playground? She gets lost all the time! And what if *she* had been the one to wet her pants at school?

The world would come to an end. Her world, anyway. For a while.

I feel really terrible now.

I never meant for this to happen. But it happened anyway!

"It's okay," Marco Adair whispers to me. "You didn't know."

"Ms. Sanchez, Ms. Sanchez," Cynthia says, waving her hand in the air as if she has something really urgent to say.

Ms. Sanchez sighs. "Yes, Miss Harbison, Miss Harbison?"

"Iggy probably can't even read," Cynthia says, like she just won an argument. "Anyway, he's the one who strayed into our herd."

She said "our herd!" Maybe while I've been reading about Merlyn and the geese, as well as all the other cool animals in *The Sword in the Stone*, Cynthia's been reading some other animal book. Probably about magic ponies or something.

"And *us girls* didn't do anything wrong," Cynthia finishes, folding her arms across her chest. "So I think the boys should write the I'm-sorry-letters, and us girls can hear the funny story."

"It's 'we girls,' not 'us girls,'" Ms. Sanchez informs her. "You would say, 'We can hear,' not 'Us can hear,' wouldn't you? That's the test. But sorry, ladies. It's not going to work that way. This class is a unit—or 'a herd,' if you prefer. It's not two teams, the boys against the girls. So get out your best pens, if you please, and I'll pass out some nice paper for you to write on. Iggy's parents can read him your notes, if he can't read them himself. I'll write a few vocabulary words on the board to help get you started," she adds.

My dad would call that "throwing us a bone."

"And then lunch?" Jared Matthews asks, sounding hopeful.

"Oh. About lunch," Ms. Sanchez says, as if Jared just reminded her of something important. "You are all marching out onto that playground as soon as the lunch buzzer sounds, and you're picking up *every scrap of toilet paper you can find*. And any other litter, as well. After that, you can wash your hands thoroughly, and *then* eat your lunch."

"But the best food will be gone in the cafeteria," Kevin cries.

"That's true," Ms. Sanchez says in a thoughtful way, as she examines her shiny fingernails. "I'm sure there will be *something* left, though. No one will starve."

And she's usually so nice.

This is all my fault—no matter *what* Marco says.

And my stomach is already growling!

"*Iggy*," Ms. Sanchez writes on the white board. "*Apologize*." "*Sincerely*."

The entire third grade flock, or herd, sighs as if it were one giant creature.

And we start to write our notes to poor wet Iggy.

✳ 10 ✳

UH-OH

I jump into the back seat of Mom's car about three minutes after school lets out. There is a long line of cars waiting at the curb. They all have their lights on and wipers going, even though it's still daytime. It has just started to rain.

I am *so* glad Mom said she would pick me up today. I didn't want the guys in my class griping again about what happened this morning.

I'm gonna end up with *no* friends, at this rate.

"Don't get me wet, EllWay, or you'll be sowwy," Alfie warns.

That's *"you'll be sorry"* in Alfie-speak.

"What's *your* problem?" I ask, wrestling with my seat belt. "What's her problem?" I ask Mom when Alfie doesn't answer me.

My sister looks like a grouchy cartoon character with a little black storm cloud over her head—

which matches today perfectly, now that I think about it. Alfie's arms are folded across her chest. She is slumped in her car seat like a rag doll. She kicked off one of her sneakers, too.

Uh-oh. That's never a good sign. I hope it didn't go out the car window.

"Talk to your brother, Alfie," Mom says, signaling to pull into the traffic. "I'm too busy trying to drive in this crazy rain to explain what happened."

"I wanna go home," Alfie says, trying to kick the back of Mom's seat, which luckily is a good eight inches from Alfie's toes. "No chores! No chores, Mom," she says, wriggling in her car seat. She aims another kick Mom's way.

"Don't do that," I tell Alfie. "It's dangerous. And you're acting like a baby."

That's the worst insult you can give her.

"You can't tell me what to do, EllWay," Alfie says. "You're not the boss of me."

"I don't even want to be the boss of you," I inform her. "Where are we going?" I ask Mom. I'm hoping for a surprise trip to a drive-through, but that hardly ever happens.

Mom and Dad want us to have all kinds of experiences. Even fast food ones.

Only not very often.

"We're headed back to the arts and crafts store, and then I need to swing by the library," Mom says, not even looking at me in the rear view mirror. That's how nervous she is about driving in the rain—or how angry she is at having to return to that store. It drives Mom nuts how messy the shelves are. She's a very neat lady.

She could organize the world if she ever got the chance.

"But I thought you got everything you needed for Alfie's goldfish costume," I remind her. "You already started making it, didn't you?"

"Miss Nancy decided Alfie would do better in another role," Mom tells me, her voice sounding a little tight. "Our Miss Alfie was saying everyone's lines for them, it seems. And she had some trouble settling down."

"Yeah. Miss Nancy cheated the rehearsal," Alfie says, pouncing on Mom's words.

"Cheated *at* the rehearsal," I correct her. "Because you can't cheat a rehearsal, Alfie. That doesn't make any sense."

"EllRay," Mom says to me from the front seat. "You're not helping."

"Did that stuff really happen?" I ask Alfie. "You saying other kids' lines?"

I'm pretty sure she's ready to talk now. Getting her to stop up will be the hard part.

"Well, I knowed 'em all, and the other kids didn't," my sister says. "Not fast enough, anyway. So Miss Nancy said I have to be the *red bird*," Alfie tells me, almost spitting out the last two words. "Just because I was saying all the lines, and maybe bothering my neighbor. It's so she can keep an eye on me, Miss Nancy says. But I don't *wanna* be the red bird. The red bird comes first, and then she just stands there like—like a *baby*. I wanna be the goldfish and come last."

"I think you 'just standing there' is the idea, Alfie," Mom says. "And it's not up to you. It's up to Miss Nancy," she adds—from the safety of the front seat, remember.

Thanks, Mom.

"There are nine characters," Mom continues. "Not counting the teacher and the children in the story. So you're lucky you're in the skit at all, especially after disrupting the rehearsal the way you did."

"What's a skit?" Alfie asks, starting to get mad all over again.

"It's, like, a little play," I tell her. "A short one."

"But this is gonna be a *big* play," Alfie argues as Mom pulls into the arts and crafts store's shiny black parking lot. "And I'm *not gonna be the red bird*. I'm telling you that much wight now."

Right now.

"Then close your eyes when we get to the red tissue paper aisle, young lady," Mom tells her, handing me a ladybug umbrella. Like that's gonna happen. "Because I don't want any unpleasant scenes in the store."

"Then I'll make a *pleasant* scene," I hear Alfie mutter once Mom is out of the car.

Uh-oh, part two.

Dad gets home late from work a couple of Wednesday nights each month because of some meeting they have in the geology department of his college. Tonight he has gotten home even later than usual, because rain messed up the traffic.

It's almost my bedtime, and I've been looking at this really cool book Mom let me check out of the library this afternoon. The book is the equipment for my Diego Romero Spare Friend Plan that I'm gonna try to pull off tomorrow at school.

If anyone is still speaking to me, that is.

Dad has just finished eating the dinner Mom heated up for him. But instead of watching the news, he wants to talk to me. I guess I'm the news, tonight.

Uh-oh, part three.

"Come on down to my office, son," he has just called up the stairs.

About ten maybe-bad things I've done leap into my brain—and also one or two for-sure-bad things. I did them by accident, but what difference does that make to Dad? They still happened.

"Ooh, busted," Alfie says from her darkened room, as I walk past her partly open door.

"You're supposed to be asleep," I inform her.

"I'm too angwy to sleep," she says.

Angry.

"You think you have problems *now*," I say over my shoulder, because—I'd give anything to have a *Brown Bear, Brown Bear* kind of problem.

Being a red bird instead of a goldfish? Big deal!

Wait until she learns about the *real* world.

"Take a seat, EllRay," Dad says from behind his desk, which has several large sparkling rocks sitting on it. It's like he's a king sitting on his throne, surrounded by a wall of crystals.

Wait. Those rocks aren't *that* big.

I know I'm in some kind of trouble, though. Mom probably heard about all the stuff that happened today at school but decided to let Dad handle it when he got home.

That must be it.

Things will go better for me if I take the first step, I decide. "Look," I say to my dad, gripping the arms of my chair like that's going to save me. "Is this about the punishment we got at lunch for making that big mess in the playground during recess? Is that why you wanted to see me? Because we picked it all up. Every scrap of paper."

Dad looks at me, his head tilted a little.

"No, wait," I say quickly. "Is this about Iggy getting so scared that he wet his pants? Because we apologized for that. We wrote him twenty-five fancy I'm-sorry letters, with correct spelling and everything. Even though he probably can't even read. Well, twenty-four letters," I correct myself. "Because one of the girls was absent today. I forget her name."

Now, Dad's looking a little confused. Like— *Iggy? Iggy who?*

So that's not it. "Is this about the Curse of the Mummy Zombie thing?" I babble on, as if my mouth is not connected to my brain in any way. "Because I didn't make up the 'curse' part, Dad. That was Major's idea. And it wasn't 'curse' like a swear. I *did* make up the mummy zombie thing, but I had a really good reason. I had *good intentions*," I add, remembering an expression Dad sometimes uses.

Parents like it when you quote what they say, even though they've already heard it before. Obviously.

By this point, the expression on Dad's face is

impossible to read. It almost looks like—like he's about to laugh? But that can't be right.

"Wait. Is this about the toilet paper I took to school?" I ask, using up my last idea. "Because I can pay for it out of my allowance!"

"The *toilet paper*?" Dad echoes. "You'd better just stop talking, son. I only wanted us to catch up a little. We haven't had any time alone together in days. But obviously, there's been a lot going on." And he leans back in his chair, inspecting me like I'm some surprising new specimen.

What have I done?

"We don't really need to talk," I jibber-jabber, wishing I could delete the past few minutes from my dad's memory bank. Wipe it clean. "Everything's good. Really! At school, I mean. *And* at home. It's good everywhere, in fact. Good, good, good!"

"Oh, it is, is it?" Dad says, like it's not really a question. "Well, why don't you tell me about the Curse of the Mummy Zombie anyway, son? I could use a good laugh about now. And we can move on to the story about the punishment at school, and then you can tell me about little Izzy's wet pants."

"Iggy," I mumble.

"Excuse me?" Dad asks.

"It was *Iggy* who wet his pants," I say, staring at my bare feet. They look so happy, so innocent! It's as if they're not attached to the rest of miserable me. "He's in the first grade, Dad."

I'm gonna be here *forever.*

And Dad's never going to understand about me needing a new spare friend by Friday, which is sure to come up.

Man, I hope I don't start crying.

But there is no other way out of this tangled-up crystal maze, so I start talking.

BABY TALK THURSDAY

"How come the wind always blows after it rains?" I ask my mom. We have just dropped off Alfie at Kreative Learning and Daycare.

It is Thursday, the day after my toilet paper disaster, and the day before Alfie's big show. Wow, I'm glad I'm not Miss Nancy today. Wait—I'm *always* glad I'm not Miss Nancy! But especially today, when she's facing one of the few rehearsals left before tomorrow's *Brown Bear, Brown Bear* disaster.

Alfie is still saying "No way!" to the whole red bird thing.

"Good question about the wind, honey," Mom says, glancing out the car window at the bending trees and skittering leaves. "You know, I always picture a rainstorm as a beautiful lady sweeping through her castle," she says. "Maybe the swish of her skirts creates a breeze as it follows her out the door."

Yeah, right, I think, trying not to make a face. I'll keep that theory to myself, if anyone asks at school. Especially during science this morning.

But that fancy explanation is pure Mom.

I hug my backpack to my chest. Inside is the big library book, wrapped every which way in aluminum foil in case it starts raining again.

I am taking no chances today.

Okay, yes, I am basically sneaking it into school. And that is against the law at our house.

1. Library books are expensive, Mom says. And the librarians work hard ordering them, and getting them ready to be checked out.

2. It is a privilege to borrow library books.

3. That's why you have to pay a fine if you bring them back late.

4. And if you damage or lose a library book, you have to pay for it. It will cost more than if you just went to the store and bought a new one, too, because of all that librarian work.

Am I *asking* for trouble?

No, I am not. I do have a plan, though. I have given up trying to convince Jason Leffer what a great-idea guy I am. Instead, I am now trying for Diego Romero, the kid who likes books. Books about cars.

He can be my new spare friend.

This library book is perfect for Diego! It's all *about* cars. It has a gold race car on the front, and lots of really cool pictures inside. But it has writing, too. Diego likes writing. We can look at the book during together recess and lunch. I'll just kind of surprise him with it.

And then later, after I invite Diego to Alfie's show tomorrow night, I can teach him some of the fun stuff *I* like to do—like play *Die, Creature, Die*. He will then be the *new-and-improved* Diego Romero.

Once we're friends, I won't be stranded every time Corey goes to swim practice, or Kevin decides to mooch around with his neighbors instead of with me.

"EllRay?" Mom says, giving me a funny look in the rearview mirror.

"Hmm?" I say, still thinking about hanging with Diego at recess, and about him unwrapping the book. I can't wait to see the look on his face!

"We're here," she tells me. "At school," she adds, as if I might need more of a clue.

"Okay. Good," I say, escaping from my seatbelt. I open the car door, get out, and lug my too-heavy backpack after me. *Ugh.* "See ya," I shout through the car window, waving bye to my mom.

Out on the playground, the girls in my class are acting extra goofy today—as if the beautiful rain lady sweeping her skirts through the castle got *them* all worked up, too. The boys are kind of standing back and watching the girls, for once.

Girls-acting-goofy just happens sometimes—for no known reason. They are like stampeding cattle in a cowboy movie, only smaller. Fads happen a lot with girls, too. In fact, the girls in my class run through fads so fast that by the time you realize one is happening, it's old news—and another fad has taken its place.

Pink Day? They had that before Christmas. No announcements or anything.

Skipping Day? Been there, saw that. The girls even tried skipping in class, until Ms. Sanchez said no. She said a few other things, too.

Don't-Say-"Boy"-Day? The girls had that one, only nobody noticed until it was almost over. They mostly ignore us boys *every* day, it seems to me.

So what fad is it going to be today?

"Goin' onna fwing, EllWay," Cynthia says, running toward the swing. There's a pink sweater wrapped around her head.

"Yeah," Heather says, racing after her. "Goo-goo, gah-gah! Toopid *boy*," she adds, pointing at me.

At me! What did *I* do?

Today, I mean.

Next to the girls' picnic table, three of them are clustered together, cooing at one another. "You so cute!"

"No, *you* so cute."

"Widdle babies," Fiona chimes in, hugging the other two.

The boys are watching this with nauseated expressions on their faces. I join them. "Hey. What's

up with them?" I ask, clunking my backpack onto the table.

I'll see if anyone is still talking to me after what happened yesterday.

"Kry says it's Baby Talk Thursday," Kevin reports, frowning. "Only I don't think *she's* doing it much. And Emma and Annie Pat can't decide if they even want to."

I laugh. "I thought it was Wear Your Sweater on Your Head Day," I say, trying out a joke.

"That's supposed to be a baby hat Cynthia has on," Kevin says, serious as anything. It's as if he is interpreting the girls to us—like some kind of goofy puzzle-solving scientist.

Kevin is not taking his worried eyes off those girls, in fact.

But me? I'm *relieved* it's Baby Talk Thursday! After all, just about every day has to be something if you're in the third grade at Oak Glen Primary School.

Hurt Feelings Day.

Scared About That Test Day.

Emma's Birthday Day.

So if this wasn't Baby Talk Thursday, it might be Thanks a Lot, EllRay! Day. And everyone would still be mad at me.

But because of the girls, we have officially "moved on," as Ms. Sanchez would say.

"Aren't you gonna eat anything?" my friend Corey Robinson asks, eyeing my backpack. Corey is always hungry, because of the swimming.

"I guess not until later," I say. I don't want any-one seeing the library book yet—or even spotting the aluminum foil it is wrapped in. Aluminum foil inside a kid's backpack usually means something yummy is inside the foil.

Like leftover birthday cake!

My mouth starts watering for a turquoise-blue frosting rose.

"Shove over. I want a front row seat for this," Marco says to me, but in a friendly way. I make room for him on the bench.

Two girls skip by, arm-in-arm. "We fwying, Marco!" one of them calls over her shoulder—as if she's showing off just for him.

"They're frying?" Marco asks, leaning forward like he just missed something.

"I think she said they're *flying*," Major tells him. "But I don't know for sure."

"How long are they gonna keep this up?" Diego wonders aloud.

"Probably all day, knowing them," I say. I try not to sound too overjoyed.

But if the girls *do* act like babies for the entire

day, then I'm out of trouble for sure! Because their being babies will soak up all the attention around here. And that's a fact.

It's kind of hard to know how to act around all this baby stuff, though. That's the only bad thing about today so far.

Are we boys supposed to ignore it?

Or go along with it?

Or argue with it?

Or wrap sweatshirts around our own heads and start making fun of it?

"Let's see what Ms. Sanchez has to say," I tell the other guys at the table. "I have the feeling babies aren't really her thing."

"Not yet, anyway," Corey says. "At least not crawling around her classroom, if that's what they've got planned."

"Yeah," I agree as the buzzer sounds. And we start for class, dodging a couple of skipping, babbling girl-babies.

Geez, what a break.

Maybe this is my lucky day!

✳ **12** ✳

HIGH PRESSURE SYSTEM

"Settle down, everyone," Ms. Sanchez says after she has taken attendance and put on her science apron. It's the sight of that apron that got us excited, because she usually plans really fun experiments for us to do. And the ones that don't work out the exact way she planned can be even better. Messier, but better.

Which is why she wears the apron.

"Now, you may have noticed how windy it is outside," Ms. Sanchez begins, perching on the front of her desk, as usual.

"Goo-goo, gah-gah," Heather murmurs, swapping baby glances with Cynthia.

"Shh," Annie Pat whispers, scowling. She and Emma want to be scientists when they grow up, and they probably think Heather and Cynthia are trying to mess with the lesson. Which they are.

"Shh, yourself," Cynthia whispers back, shrugging to show how bored she is with Annie Pat—and with science, for that matter.

"So," Ms. Sanchez continues, "does anyone know *why* it's windy outside?"

Wow, I think, and my eyes are big with surprise. That is just what I was asking my mom!

Stanley Washington's hand shoots up.

"Yes, Stanley?" Ms. Sanchez says.

"It's windy because the weather-guesser on TV *said* it would be windy," he says.

"I think they prefer to be called *meteorologists*, not *weather-guessers*," Ms. Sanchez says, laughing. "And before anyone asks, the term 'meteorology' comes from an ancient Greek word that refers to any event taking place in the sky. That's how meteors got their name, I suppose, since they are one thing that can happen in the sky. But what *weather-related events* take place in our earth's atmosphere?"

Emma raises her hand. "Rain?" she says after Ms. Sanchez calls on her.

Emma can make things sound like questions even when they aren't.

"That's right," Ms. Sanchez says. "And snow, and—"

"And UFOs," Jared Matthews says, excited enough to interrupt.

"Like, with space aliens inside?" Heather asks, forgetting for a second to be a baby.

"Raise your hands, please," Ms. Sanchez reminds them. "And let's leave UFOs and space aliens for another lesson. Probably not science," she adds, laughing again. "We've got our hands full today with the weather. We were talking about— "

"*The wind,*" a few kids say together, finishing her sentence the way she sometimes wants us to. We can always tell when.

"Right," Ms. Sanchez says. "And it's windy today because the air pressure is trying to adjust itself after the rain. It likes to be nice and balanced. So the air pressure is trying to move from the *high pressure system* of the cold, heavy rainstorm we had last night to a lighter and and more normal *low pressure system* today. And that's what is making the wind blow."

Annie Pat raises her hand. "But you can't really see air pressure, right?" she asks after Ms. Sanchez calls on her. "Except when the wind blows?"

"That's right, Annie Pat," Ms. Sanchez says, smiling at her. "But you are seeing the *effects* of air pressure when the wind blows, not seeing the air pressure itself. Sometimes you can feel air pressure, though. Did any of you ever get to fly in an airplane when you were a baby?"

Lots of hands shoot up into the air. Even mine, because we flew to see my grandparents once. I don't remember it, but I've seen the pictures.

There still used to be paper photographs when I was a baby. Pictures weren't just on people's phones or cameras, like now.

"And did one or two of you get an earache in the plane?" Ms. Sanchez asks.

Corey raises his hand. "My mom said I did, once," he reports, sounding proud. "She said I screamed and screamed when we were landing, and people gave her dirty looks. So she gave me a bottle."

"Ooo," a couple of the girls say. One of them pats Corey's back, as if his plane just now landed, and he might still need comforting.

Next, they'll probably want him to join their goo-goo, gah-gah baby club.

Good luck with *that*.

"Your poor little ears hurt because of the air pressure change in the plane's cabin," Ms. Sanchez tells Corey. "It's something babies grow out of, thank goodness. But that's what we'll be talking about this morning, people: air pressure. And we have three air pressure experiments to get through. So come on up here, Cynthia," she says. "And Corey, too. And—how about EllRay? We need three students with good sets of lungs to blow up a few balloons."

"Don't wanna," Cynthia says, turning into a baby again. She sinks down in her chair like she's melting. **"WAH–H–H,"** she fake-cries, peeking around to see how we're taking it.

"I didn't ask if you wanted to, Miss Harbison," Ms. Sanchez says. She still sounds pretty cheerful, in spite of everything. "And remember," our teacher adds. "This is a science class, not a drama class."

She says that when someone—usually one of the girls—starts acting up.

Wait until Alfie is in her class!

"But I'm feepy," Cynthia says in baby talk, cradling her arms on her desk and putting her head down for a pretend nap.

"Poor widdle baby," Heather says, petting her arm. "So *cute.*"

"Not cute at all," Ms. Sanchez says, snapping out the words. "And *right—now,*" she adds, clicking both fingers as she speaks. "Also, no more baby talk, if you please, ladies—or I'll send out for a few jars of strained lima beans, and we'll see how you like *that.* Hurry," she adds, her usually warm voice turning cool. "Tick-tock."

Uh-oh. There's a high pressure system building up.

Cynthia hurries.

And we begin our three air pressure experiments.

"I liked the trick where Jared and Emma jammed their straw into the potato," Stanley says as we paw through our cubbies, getting out snacks for morning recess.

"We did it using air pressure," Annie Pat points out, shrugging her arms into her jacket. "And it was an experiment, not a trick."

"If you say so," Stanley says, laughing.

"I *do* say so," Annie Pat tells him.

"I liked the trick where Ms. Sanchez made the hard-boiled egg squeeze into the bottle," Jared says. "Like magic. *POP!* "

"Using air pressure," Annie Pat says again.

Give it up, I think, hiding a smile. I zip up my dark blue San Diego Padres sweatshirt and give my backpack—and the hidden library book inside—a friendly pat. Ms. Sanchez says that the meteorological event happening outside now is that it's drizzling. I can't risk getting drizzle all over the book.

I'll wait until lunch to bring it outside, but it has to happen today.

Because I am running out of time.

Drizzly mornings are perfect for kickball and foursquare, though—and also for yelling and running around. My legs are itching to run, in fact.

"Did you eat your snack yet?" Marco asks, jamming a few little plastic bags into his sweatshirt pouch.

"Most of it," I admit.

"EllRay likes to chow down before school even starts," Corey tells Marco, laughing. "You know. Get it over with so he can play more. He even eats what he's gonna have for lunch, sometimes."

"Hey. I eat half *my* lunch before school," Major says to me, amazed at the coincidence.

"Huh," I say, grinning at him. "I should try that, so I don't starve by the time school is out. Anyway, Corey should talk," I tell Major and Marco, giving Corey a shove. "He's *always* eating. His mom packs him twice as much food as normal, that's the thing. And it's all healthy."

"It's true," Corey tells Marco and Major, a smile spreading across his friendly, freckled face. "I love to eat. And my mom says if you eat healthy, you can eat more."

I look around to see where Diego is, but he's probably already outside, playing.

Your life is about to change for the better, Diego Romero. So get ready!

"I'll share," Marco tells me, keeping his voice low.

"Huh?"

"I'll share my snack with you if you're hungry," he says, repeating the offer. "I've got string cheese in one bag, and some mini muffins in the other bag. My mom made 'em. And I brought some of my knights to play with, too."

"I like all that stuff," I admit as we churn out the door.

Okay. My stomach is officially gurgling now.

"You even like the knights?" Marco shouts over the noise in the hall. "I've got a couple of dragons, too!"

"He does have dragons," Major says. "He'll even share."

"I *guess* I like them," I say as we run outside. I scan the playground first for my future friend Diego, who is nowhere to be seen. Then I look for Mr. Havens. He is handing out kickballs slowly, like he's a Santa Claus who is running out of presents.

Are any kickballs going to be left?

And if there are, will Mr. Havens give me one— after what happened yesterday?

I don't think so.

"I'll take a muffin, I guess," I tell Marco, shrugging. "If you really mean it."

"Why wouldn't I mean it?" Marco asks, pulling a plastic bag from his sweatshirt pouch. He hands me not one but *two* little muffins. Yum! I peel the paper off one and cram it into my mouth.

"C'mon, you guys," Corey yells. "It looks like there's only one kickball left—and we gotta score it!"

"Race ya," Major shouts.

"Yeah. Race ya," Marco says.

"Mmph," I say, sputtering muffin crumbs.

And all four of us take off running across the wet playground, our sneakers flashing.

✳ 13 ✳

KEEP-AWAY

"The sun is shining," Kry says at lunchtime, as if we can't see out the window ourselves.

But we don't mind it when she tells us obvious stuff. Everyone likes Kry.

I turn my back to the other kids in the cubby area. I wiggle the foil-wrapped library book out of my backpack. The book is bigger than I remember. But it's flat—compared to yesterday's lumpy roll of toilet paper, anyway.

I slide the wrapped-up library book under my sweatshirt.

There. Do I look perfectly normal?

No, I do not. In fact, I look like I am wearing a bulletproof vest under my sweatshirt, like some guy on a TV show. Or maybe I look like I'm wearing a thin suit of armor. Marco will think I'm a secret knight—but a lot bigger than the plastic ones he sneaks to school.

It's cool being bigger than *something*.

But Diego is gonna think this book is great, so it's all worth it.

I'm just one small step away from having my plan come true. I *am* going to be the recess king! I will invite Diego to come to Alfie's show tomorrow night. Then we'll all go out for pizza—or ice cream. Whichever he likes best.

Especially if it's what Alfie likes best, too.

We'll be friends *for sure*. And then no matter how busy Corey is with swim practice, or how much fun Kevin is having with the neighbor kids, I'll always have a cool spare friend to hang with.

I can work on digging up a spare-spare friend after that, once I rest up from finding this one.

I don't want to brag, but I think I am turning into a good idea guy.

Outside, puffy white clouds are bouncing around the cold blue sky the same way that we kids are bouncing around the playground. "Hey EllRay. Over here," Kevin says from one of the boys' picnic tables. And so I hold the library book in place and trot over, covering my chest the best I can with my lunch bag.

Most of the guys are already at the table. The ones who aren't eating in the cafeteria, anyway. But my theory is that you miss out on too much playground time when you eat in the cafeteria. It just doesn't make sense.

This is Oak Glen, California, after all. Not the North Pole.

Even Jason is sitting at the picnic table, but he's been pretty much ignoring me since yesterday. Oh, well.

"EllRay's running funny," Jared calls out, laughing in his *haw-haw* way.

"Like a girl," Stanley adds. But *he wishes* he could run like Kry Rodriguez does.

Well, he doesn't really wish that. But he is not as good a runner as Kry.

I'm just saying.

"I'm trying to stay warm," I pretend-explain, still hugging my sweatshirt—and the book—to my chest. I squeeze in between Diego and Kevin. Diego is sitting at the end of the bench, which is perfect. I try to paw through my lunch bag with my right hand, while still holding the foil-wrapped library book to my chest with my left hand.

It's at a time like this when a person could use three hands, in my opinion.

All that's left of my lunch is a banana, some cheese squares, and three oatmeal cookies that are so small an elf could munch them down without any problem. That's Mom's latest thing, making food small, especially treats. So an actual person has to eat a ton of them for it to come out right.

Dang, I'm hungry.

But I am also excited, because of my excellent plan.

I slide a miniature oatmeal cookie into my mouth, and the book under my sweatshirt slips a little.

"Watcha got there?" Jared asks, spying a triangle corner of the foil-wrapped book. "Treats?"

Jared is always hungry. Well, most of us guys are. We're like sharks, who are "eating machines," Annie Pat tells us. She wants to be a fish scientist when she grows up, so she knows stuff like that.

As I said before, the best things to eat at Oak Glen Primary School—like leftover birthday cake—usually come wrapped in aluminum foil. So Jared thinks he's really onto something.

"It *is* treats," he tells the whole table of boys. "And EllRay's hogging."

"I am not hogging," I say, my heart starting to thud.

This is not going the way I thought it would, that's for sure. Oh, it's not going *terrible*, because what do I care if the guys in my class discover I checked out a library book about cars? It's not like I sneaked in a Barbie encyclopedia or something.

Which Alfie would just love, by the way.

This was going to be a private thing between Diego and me, but I decide to get it over with. "Look. I'll show you," I tell everyone at the table. I pull out the foil-wrapped book from under my sweatshirt. I start to unwrap a corner while I hold the book up for everyone to see. I sneak a look at Diego. "It's this really cool—"

"Gingerbread!" Jared says, reaching across the table like lightning, and grabbing the foil-wrapped package from my hands. "A whole slab of it! And EllRay wasn't even gonna share!"

Jared untangles himself from the picnic table bench and takes off with his prize, *my book*, shouting, "Gingerbread!" He is holding the library book over his head like a trophy as he runs. Stanley, Jason, and Kevin take off after him, laughing.

Gingerbread? He *saw* part of the cover! And that book's as hard as a rock.

Well, as hard as a book, anyway.

A *library* book.

Taken out in *my name*.

Dollar signs, and scoldings from my parents—*and the librarian*—pop into my head like cartoon thought-balloons. And before I know it, I'm chasing my book's kidnappers, even though chasing Jared is probably exactly what he wants me to do.

But I can't help it.

I don't even look to see if anyone's following me.

"HAW, HAW, HAW," Jared donkey-laughs again, seeing me come after him. He starts shedding pieces of aluminum foil as he runs. He doesn't even care about the litter lecture we're sure to get from Mr. Havens, who is still the substitute recess monitor. I think maybe the regular guy ran away from school.

Where is Mr. Havens, by the way?

"Hey," Jared is shouting now, shaking the library book in his big pink hand as he runs. "What it this, anyway? A *book*?"

He sounds angry, like I really put one over on him.

"Yeah, it's a book, *Einstein*," I yell, pounding after him. "A library book. You can't eat it. So give it here!"

Jared stops for a minute, waggling the book as he holds it out toward me. "Come and get it," he says, in a mocking voice.

And then he hurls it through the air to Stanley, his personal assistant.

"Keep-away!" Jared cries.

"Keep-away," Stanley echoes.

Okay, I think, crouching low like a ninja as I plan my attack. Keep-away is something that is supposed to be a game. Except really, it's usually just big kids being mean to smaller kids.

And unfortunately, today, I happen to be the smaller kid involved.

A really fair "game," right?

Where's Merlyn when you need him? He could turn Jared into a bug!

The script for keep-away never changes. There are only three sure-fire lines.

1. There's *"Keep—away!"* and
2. *"Give it here,"* and
3. "Come and get it!"

That's about it.

Stanley tosses my library book to Jason, and its pages flutter as it flies through the air. "Come and get it," Jason shouts, barely holding onto the book—even though the grassy hill is muddy from the rain.

As if he can read my mind, Jason opens up the book and puts it on his head like a funny hat. "*La-la-la-la-la,*" he chants, prancing around. "Look at me! I'm so *beautiful*. Hope I don't drop this thing. And thanks for gettin' me in trouble yesterday, dude," he adds, being Jason again.

Jason Leffer, who was going to be my new spare friend.

"I didn't mean to," I say, barely aware of the kids moving up behind me. "How did I know that little guy was gonna spring a leak and bring us all down? Come on, Jason. Give it here," I say, holding out my puny Tyrannosaurus-rex hands.

"Keep-away," Jason jeers, tossing the book back to Jared.

It cartwheels through the air in slow motion.

And that's when the kids behind me spring into action. "Get it," Corey shouts, making a side run around Stanley and heading toward Jared. Jared is not a very fast thinker in situations like this.

He's big, but he is "definitely not quarterback material," as my dad would probably put it. We watch a lot of football together.

And out from behind my other side sprint Nate, Major, Marco, Kevin, and Diego. That's a total of six kids on my side. *Six whole kids.*

Seven, counting me. Seven against three!

I had no idea I had so many friends.

There's no time to feel happy about it, though. "Come and get it," Jared shouts for the second time.

But he is now keeping a wary eye on the line of fierce-faced kids heading his way.

Stanley looks like he has changed his mind about the whole keep-away thing, but Jason's still in. *Wow*, he must really be mad at me. "Throw it here," Jason yells to Jared. He claps his hands a couple of times, to warm them up for the big catch, I guess.

So much for pizza and ice cream, dog. And for me teaching you the secrets to *Die, Creature, Die*.

"Don't come any closer," Jared warns my friends, but they creep toward him anyway, like silent warriors. I'm heading his way, too.

We approach our enemy. Like I said, my loyal army consists of:

1. Corey Robinson.
2. Kevin McKinley.
3. Nate Marshall.
4. Major Donaldson.
5. Marco Adair.
6. Diego Romero, my maybe new spare friend.
7. And me, EllRay Jakes.

"Stop right there, or I'm gonna throw this dumb book on the ground," Jared shouts. His eyes look a little wild.

"You can't," Diego says. "That's a library book! It's against the law!"

Like, *"That's that, dude."*

Only that *isn't* that. Not with Jared Matthews, it isn't.

"Oh, yeah?" Jared says. "Well, it's not against *my* law. Watch this, stupid-heads," he says.

And he opens up the book as wide as it will go, hurls it onto the playground, and grinds it into the grass and mud with one gigantic sneaker. *"Take that,"* he yells at the book. At the book! How messed-up can you get? "Now, what are you gonna do about it?" he yells at us.

And he beckons us toward him with both hands. Like, *"Bring it. "*

And so, even though this was not what we planned, and even though I, for one, do not have a whole lot to bring, we do.

We bring it, I mean.

✳ **14** ✳

"FIGHT! FIGHT!"

Seven of us is more than three of them. Jared, Jason, and Stanley. So my side is lucky—in numbers, anyway. But the three other guys are larger than us in size and fury. Jared is just plain big and angry, even though I'm the one who should be mad. Stanley is tall. And, as I mentioned once before, Jason is kind of on the chunky side, even if it is pure muscle, like he says.

Plus, Jason's probably got the whole pay-back thing revving him up, because of our toilet paper adventure yesterday.

All ten of us start to circle, not taking our eyes off one another. And as we pace, the circle gets smaller.

It's getting pretty intense around here.

Jared Matthews is giving me the stink-eye.

Armpit Noise King Marco is scowling at stringbean Stanley and his very plaid shirt.

Stanley is darting his meanest look from Marco to Major, then back to Marco again. He probably can't remember which one's which.

Buzz-cut Jason is staring hard at Corey Robinson. Corey is pale but determined-looking under the three hundred freckles on his face. It sometimes seems like Corey is made out of pipe cleaners, but the whole class knows how strong he is from all that swimming.

It looks like Diego Romero is "reading Jared like a book," as my Dad sometimes says. I think that means Diego knows what's up with Jared and his hot-headed ways.

And Nate's red rooster crest of hair is almost standing at attention as he shifts his furious glare from Jared to Jason to Stanley. Nate's hands are even clenched like rooster claws. He is ready to pounce.

Yoo-hoo! Mr. Havens! Where are you? Getting a nice energy drink?

Our circle keeps getting smaller, like it's a spring winding tighter and tighter. It's about to go **BOING**. Pretty soon there will be no place left to go, and nothing else to do but fight—which means we'll be busted big-time.

Listen. *Running in the halls* is against the rules at Oak Glen Primary School.

Not rinsing out your milk carton before recycling it is against the rules.

You can probably guess how they feel about playground brawls around here!

I'll admit it. Part of me wouldn't *mind* fighting, not after what Jared did to my very expensive library book, which, P.S., I will now have to pay for. It wasn't the book's fault that it wasn't a sweet and crumbly slab of gingerbread, was it?

But I don't like the getting-in-trouble part that comes *after* a fight.

Not to mention what will happen to me at home. Because basically, you can at least double any scolding I get at school, and you'll be close to what happens when my mom and dad get hold of any bad news about me.

Also, fighting won't help my wrecked library book any, will it?

I think about mom and dad. I also think about how boring it is, circling around and around like the ants in *The Sword in the Stone*, who are always getting ready for war—even though they don't know why. I try to plot how to get out of this goofy situation without looking like a chicken or a fool. But just when my brain starts to **TICK, TICK, TICK,** trying to come up with an idea, the dreaded words come floating across the playground. "Fight! Fight!"

The older boys have spotted us. And almost *all* the lunch kids on the playground race toward us. Nobody wants to miss a moment of this stupendous, ten-person battle, even though we are only third-graders.

If it actually happens, our fight will make Oak Glen Primary School history.

And not in a good way.

"Fight! Fight!"

Okay, here is the embarrassing truth about the whole **"FIGHT! FIGHT!"** thing.

1. If the kids who are mad are still throwing stink-eyes and making threats after five minutes, not pounding on each other, they are about ready for the whole thing to be finished, in my opinion. Not

because they're scared, but because they're over it. Face it. Other stuff is more fun. And how long can a person stay mad?

2. But then *other* kids see what's happening, and they gather. They say things like, *"Go ahead! Hit 'im!"* Because what do *those kids* care if the fighting kids get in trouble? It's just more entertainment for them!

3. That's when it's hard for fighting kids to back down, though. Even if they really *are* over the whole thing.

    Like I am here, now.

    That's when it takes guts to stop.

4. So, what's a kid supposed to do? Especially when there are no grown-ups around?

Hope that energy drink is extra good today, Mr. Havens!

And—*FWUMP.*

I'm flat on the ground.

Then, **BAM, BAM, BAM**. Other guys pile on top of me. It's like we are making a sky-high, noisy, third-grade kid sandwich.

OOF!

I can hear the older kids hooting and jeering at us.

A few of us third-graders *are* trying to fight a little, or we're pretending to. It's like we have to put on enough of a show to satisfy the older kids—even though we're so mooshed together we can barely move. I have hold of one of Jason's sticking-out ears. Corey is growling. And some other kid—

probably Jared—is twisting my sweatshirt so tight that it's like he's trying to wring me out.

And then, **FWOOSH**.

Jared seems to fly off me, leaving my sweatshirt wrinkled, but in one piece.

Corey disappears from the pile, too.

Jason, Stanley, and Kevin have been lifted off as well, and now it's easier to breathe. What is happening?

Even though I am still on the ground, I peek around for a clue.

And I see several pairs of grown-up feet.

Mr. Havens is here, hoisting kids off the pile left and right, and so is Principal James. And even Miss Myrna, the little old lady who helps out in the auditorium.

How embarrassing.

All the big kids have disappeared, of course. They seem to have melted into the playground.

And all that's left is goofy, guilty *us*.

"Okay," Principal James says. "Break it up. Break it up."

I feel like explaining to him that there isn't really anything to break up. This whole thing was just a keep-away game gone wrong! And then, when we were facing off, we kind of got forced into a fake fight by the big kids.

"I turn my back for *one minute*," Mr. Havens says, holding tight onto Marco's shoulder, as if he might run away at any second.

And go where, Mr. Havens?

I get to my feet one sore inch at a time.

"It's not your fault, Mr. Havens," Miss Myrna is saying, trying to make the second grade teacher feel better, I guess. "You were taking care of Little Miss Nosebleed, over by the swings."

Wait. They have *nicknames* for us? That's messed-up!

I wonder what *my* nickname is?

B–Z–Z–Z–Z–Z! The buzzer sounds.

"In my office, each and every one of you boys," Principal James says in a voice that tells us we'd better not argue. Like we *would*! "Miss Myrna," he adds. "Please go tell Ms. Sanchez that she'll be missing a few students for a while. I'm sure she'll be interested to hear how they spent their lunch break. Now, march," he tells us, like we're soldiers. Or prisoners, maybe. That's more like it.

"Can I get my library book?" I find the courage to ask, trying to keep my voice steady, in spite of all the trouble I'm in. "It, um, fell. It's on the ground over there," I add, pointing.

"And that, Mr. Jakes, is why we don't eat lunch with library books," Principal James says, his beard bristling. "Grab it fast, and then follow me."

So I do, and I do.

We *all* do.

We follow Principal Harry—*Hairy*—James, I mean.

Left, right. Left, right. Left, right.

Off to meet our doom.

✳ 15 ✳

BIRDS OF A FEATHER

"We covered for you yesterday, dog. So you better not tell," Jared says to me under his breath. We are making our way toward the school building, following Principal James like—well, like a bunch of bad geese who have been placed under arrest. You know, geese. Like in *The Sword in the Stone*.

"Yeah," Stanley and Jason chime in.

"Dudes. You don't have to threaten me," I say, shaking my head. "If I was going tattle on you guys, wouldn't I have already done it? Principal James asked what happened. And I didn't blab."

Jared looks like he can't remember back that far. It's been three whole minutes, after all. But hey, he's still one of the flock. Or "herd," as Cynthia would say.

"Yeah," Marco says, backing me up. "EllRay

would have already blabbed. And he *didn't*."

Corey, Kevin, and Major nod, backing him up.

Diego and Nate just keep plodding along.

"I told Principal James the book fell on the ground, remember?" I tell Jared, Stanley, and Jason, and whoever else is listening. "*I'm* the one who got yelled at for bringing a library book to lunch. *I'm* the one who's gonna have to pay it off for the next ten years. Not to mention what happens when my mom and dad find out," I add, shuddering.

"What *about* your mom and dad?" Stanley asks as we start down the hall.

"You think they're not gonna get mad at me about this?" I ask. "Have you *met* them?"

"They're kinda strict," Corey says, cluing Stanley in.

He should talk! Corey's mom runs his whole life, practically. But this is no time to pick a fight with my one-and-only friend. That would *really* mess things up.

All I wanted in the first place was *more* friends. And I wanted them bad!

I *need* more friends, so I will always have someone to hang with after school and on weekends. Someone to play video games with. Stuff is just more fun that way.

Also, this may sound weird, but I want Alfie to think I'm at least a little bit popular. I'm her *big brother*. And she'll be in kindergarten here soon. I don't want her to think Oak Glen Primary School is a tough place for us Jakes kids to make friends.

Like I said before, I look out for my little sister.

Jason doesn't seem at all interested in being my friend, though. Not after yesterday. And Diego is off in his own daydreamy world again. He never even noticed the book!

That leaves me with no one but almost-always-too-busy Corey, who I've kind of been ignoring lately. I admit it.

"Into the office," the head secretary says, shooing us with her hands.

"All ten of us?" I ask, surprised. Because usually, from what I hear, Principal James likes to talk to kids one at a time when there's trouble. It's probably so they can't all grab onto some fake story like it's a life-raft that might save them all.

"That's right," the secretary says. "Each and every one of you."

And so in we go, in clumps:

1. Jared Matthews, Stanley Washington, Kevin McKinley, and Jason Leffer.
2. Diego Romero and Nate Marshall.
3. Major Donaldson and Marco Adair.
4. And Corey and me. Or I.

There are two visitors' chairs in Principal James's office, but none of us kids sits down. Nobody wants to look that permanent, in my opinion.

"Eyes front, gentlemen," Principal James says from behind the desk. He raps his stapler on it to get our attention—which he already has, believe me.

I think he's being sarcastic, calling us "gentlemen," by the way. But it's hard to tell, with that beard on his face.

"Now, we have a problem," he begins—and I wait for him to ask who did what.

Grownups don't usually care about the "why" or "when" parts all that much.

But I don't think anyone's gonna blab.

"Birds of a feather flock together." My mom told me that once. It's an old saying from at least five hundred years ago, in England, she said. She was explaining the geese in *The Sword in the Stone* to me at the time. But I think the guys in my class are going to flock together today, too.

Especially since that's what we did yesterday.

"EllRay?" Principal James begins. "You were at the bottom of the pile, and your book got ruined. So I guess you are the injured party here. Do you have something to say?"

"I'm not injured," I tell him really fast. "I was just smooshed, that's all. Everyone was. We were only playing, see."

"I meant that your *book* was damaged," Principal James says, his glasses glittering. "Your library book—which is city property, by the way."

"Oh," I say, holding what's left of the book against my muddy sweatshirt. I am trying to think fast. "It was just an accident, like I said. The book fell," I try to explain.

"It looks like a steamroller ran over it," the principal says. "Nothing to report?"

"Nope," I say, shaking my head again.

If this was a bullying thing, I would speak right up. Maybe not here, in front of everyone. But if some kid was getting pushed around, I'd speak up for sure. You just *need* to.

Everyone knows that, nowadays.

But today, at lunch, that was just us guys "getting carried away."

That's how my mom sometimes puts it when Alfie and I are throwing pillows at each other, and we break a lamp or something. "It was on accident," Alfie always says, making everything worse—because you're supposed to say *"by accident."*

At my house, you can sometimes do stuff wrong, as long as you say it right.

"Then we'll move on to *my* problem," Principal James tells us through his beard, yanking my thoughts back to what's happening now. "Want to know what my problem is?"

"Yeah." "Sure." "I guess," a few of us mutter. The rest of us just nod or stare down at our muddy sneakers.

But Principal James isn't really waiting for our answer. "*My* problem is that I want our playground to be a nice, safe place for everyone to be," he tells us. "Both at recess, and during lunch. Right?"

"Right," one or two kids squawk. It's like they've been hypnotized into saying the correct thing.

But Principal James is not even listening. "So," he continues. "When the playground is *not* a nice, safe place for everyone, what are my options?"

For one crazy second I'm afraid Corey is going to raise his hand and ask what the word "options" means, but he doesn't. I think he may be paralyzed by fear. He has never been in this much trouble before.

You can see every freckle on his face, he is so pale.

"I *suppose* I could cancel third grade recess altogether, *forever*," Principal James says. He taps his hairy chin as he pretends to come up with this great choice. Or *option*.

Kevin squeaks, I guess at the thought of going an entire morning or afternoon without recess. Recess is his favorite part of the day! Jared nudges him to shut up.

We're not allowed to *say* "shut up" at Oak Glen, but we can nudge it.

"And for lunch," Principal James continues, "maybe I should assign each of you boys a seat in the cafeteria. You can sit boy, girl, boy, girl. And after eating, you can march straight back to class and practice your vocabulary words, instead of playing outside. How does that sound? Is *that* the solution to my problem?"

Don't answer him, I brain-wave to Cody. *It's not a real question, dog.*

Luckily, Cody is still frozen where he stands.

"For reals?" Stanley finally asks, as if all hope is lost.

"Not necessarily," Principal James says. "But I think you can see where I'm going with this," he adds. He leans forward.

Not really, I think as Major and Marco take a small step back. Because—is this what Principal James is really gonna do, or not?

"Do I have to spell it out?" our principal asks.

Spell it out. Spell it out. Spell it out, I think, now trying to brain-wave Principal James, of all people.

"Okay, here's the deal," the principal says. He

holds out his big skinny hands palms up, like he's giving us a present. "We can let what happened today slide, if—and only if—you vow never to let it happen again. No more destruction of private property on my playground. No more pile-ups. And no more fights, or I *will* crack down. And I know you know I mean it. Do you understand me? Do you *vow*?"

Jason puts his hand on his chest like he's saying the Pledge of Allegiance. "I vow," he announces in a shaky voice.

And he's not even joking, for once.

"*Dude*," Jared says, now giving *him* an elbow in the ribs.

"You have an objection, Mr. Matthews?" Principal James asks Jared.

"Nuh-uh," Jared mumbles.

"Excuse me?" the principal asks, cupping a hand to his ear.

"No objection, sir," Jared says, louder this time.

"So, vow," Principal James says.

"*We vow*," we all say in union.

"Excellent," Principal James says, getting to his

feet. "Now, you can all walk *quietly* back to class," he tells us. "Miss Myrna will accompany you. And each of you will thank her when you get there."

Nobody argues.

"Parents *may* be notified about this," the principal continues. "And you boys will miss afternoon recess today. You need to make up this morning's work. But, good news! I'll come supervise, so Ms. Sanchez can still have her break. There's no reason she should have to suffer for your bad choices."

Wait. He *might* tell our parents? That's worse than saying he *will* tell them! It means we will have to tell them first, just in case. And maybe for *no reason*.

And he's going to supervise us *in class* all during recess?

I thought we were home free—with just a scolding!

"Any problems with that? Any dissent? Any *discussion*?" Principal James asks, hand cupped to his ear again.

"Naw. We're good," Nate says, speaking for all of us.

"Excellent," Principal James says, smiling. "Until we meet again, gentlemen."

We just stand there and stare at him.

"I think that means we can leave," I finally tell everyone.

And so down the hall we go. Quietly, just like Miss Myrna tells us to do.

Man, what a terrible Thursday.

16

NERVOUS

"Pile in, honey," Mom says later that afternoon, through the partly open passenger side car window.

It has started raining again, so I am glad to do it. But when I open the rear door, I am surprised to see a wall of plastic-wrapped toilet paper between my seat and Alfie's. "I'm over here, EllWay," she calls out. "Don't wowwy."

Which means "*worry.*" Too bad Cynthia, Heather, and Fiona missed out on that one today, on Baby Talk Thursday.

Another two huge packages of TP are on the car floor in front of Alfie. They are basically blocking her in. Sweet!

"We don't even need seat-belts anymore," Alfie tells me.

"Yes, you do," Mom says from the front seat. "Buckle up," she reminds me.

"I'm buckled," I say. "You went shopping."

Now *I'm* Einstein.

"Sure did," Mom says, signaling to pull away from the curb.

"Did you get any fun stuff?" I ask. "Is it in the trunk?"

"Nuh-uh," Alfie calls out, answering the question. "This is it. And it's a present for your school!"

"Alfie," Mom pretend-scolds. "It was supposed to be a surprise. I got a few families to make donations," she explains to me.

Oh, geez.

"I'm not even *going* to kindergarten if they don't have toilet paper when I get there," Alfie announces from behind her cushiony wall. "And nobody can make me," she adds. Just for good measure, I guess.

She's pretty brave when she's inside a TP fortress.

I shrink back into my seat. "How many other families did you call?" I ask my mom.

"Oh, three or four," Mom says, her signal *TICK-TICK-TICKING* as she changes lanes. "But I left messages on a couple of other answering machines. One of the families has a big van, so they'll be picking up all the packages over the weekend. We'll surprise Principal James with it on Monday morning."

You sure will, I think, imagining the scene. Pretty soon, I'll be able to find my way to his office with a blindfold on. "*Mom*," I say, trying to sound normal. "Why?"

"How can you even ask?" Mom says, flashing me a smile in the rearview mirror. "I'm not going to let you children get tummyaches and what-not because you don't want to use the bathrooms at school."

"I never said kids were getting tummyaches," I remind her. "And those aren't even gonna fit," I mumble, looking at the plump rolls of paper. I picture the silver metal boxes that hold the waxy squares of TP we use at school.

"We'll solve each problem as it arises," Mom promises me. "Parent power, EllRay. We are here for your school! Never fear."

I chew my lower lip. One or two problems are going to come up a little sooner than she is expecting, I think. Like the truth about Oak Glen Primary School's so-called toilet paper shortage, for one.

And what happened to my expensive library book today, for two.

But I'll just let it all unroll naturally—like a really long piece of soft white paper.

What choice do I have?

"Um, listen. There's something I have to say," I tell Mom and Dad after dinner. The three of us are still sitting at the table. Alfie asked to be excused so she could squeeze in some horsie time before her bath.

"I thought there might be," Mom says. "The state you came home in."

"What? *California*?" I ask, frowning, because— what state did she *expect* me to come home in?

Dad clears his throat a couple of times.

"No. Covered in mud," Mom explains. "And looking like you lost your best friend in the world. Rough day, honey?"

If she gets any nicer, I'm gonna start crying.

Wait until she hears what *really* happened— apart from the whole mummy zombie thing, which they already know about.

1. First, there's the TP–shortage–at–school misunderstanding. Okay, fib. Okay, lie.
2. And then there's me sneaking that library book into school.
3. This is followed by the book getting ruined. Oh, and by ten of us boys getting called into Principal James's office for supposedly fighting during lunch.

Not to mention the complete failure of my spare friend goal—and what a bad example I'm setting for Alfie. You know, about making friends in primary school.

Mom's not gonna be so nice to me *then*.

"A rough *two* days," I say. I brush a few crumbs from the table into my hand. I look around, not knowing what to do with them. So I eat them.

"Want to talk about it here? Now?" Dad asks. "Or should the three of us meet in the family room in half an hour, after Alfie gets tucked into bed?"

In *half an hour*? What planet is my dad living on? Getting Alfie into bed takes forever. She is the world's slowest bath-taker, for one thing. First, you have to talk her *into* the tub. And then she won't get *out,* she's having so much fun. Also, Alfie has a ton of nighty-night routines that have to go just right, or she'll say she can't sleep.

Or let anyone else sleep, either.

But even though I'm the one who told Mom and Dad we should talk, I'm nervous about it. So I don't mind the delay.

"We can wait," I tell my dad.

"EllRay," Mom says, leaning forward as if she just got the best idea in the world. "You go talk to your little sister, okay? Just kind of ease her toward the idea of bath-time. Get her calmed down. She's all excited about the show tomorrow at Kreative Learning and Daycare."

"Listen. We all are," Dad says, and Mom starts to giggle.

"Warren," she says, giving him a look.

"I am *not* giving her a bath, even if it's an emergency," I inform my mom. "*Or* staying in the bathroom with her when she's in the tub, either. So please don't ask me to."

"Not a problem, buddy," Dad says, laughing.

"That's right, honey-bun," Mom agrees. "I'm just asking you to talk to Alfie in her room. Ask her how the *Brown Bear, Brown Bear* rehearsal went today. That sort of thing."

"I guess I could talk to her," I tell them.

Maybe I can really drag it out, I think, already plotting. *I know.* I'll ask Alfie what it's like being the red bird in the skit. I mean in the *play*.

That ought to chew up an hour or two.

With any luck, Mom and Dad will be too tired to meet later in the family room. And they will never find out what's been happening at school.

But at least I can say I tried to tell them.

✳ 17 ✳

MR. BRIGHT IDEA

"Knock, knock," I say at Alfie's bedroom door.

"Come in," Alfie says. "*I see a lellow duck looking at me*," she announces in a loud and gloomy voice as I enter her room. "That's my whole speech for tomowwow. *Supposedly*," she adds. "And then I have to just stand there quietly and pwetend I'm listening to everyone else," she finishes, shaking her head in disgust.

Yeah. *That's* gonna happen. And she's mixing up her Ls and Ys again, like she did a couple of years ago. Is it going to be Baby Talk Friday at Kreative Learning and Daycare tomorrow night?

Alfie is wearing striped leggings, a tutu, and a shrunken T-shirt. In other words, she is not ready to take a bath. Instead, she is putting two of her plastic horses to bed—but on their sides, under a tiny quilt. "Want to practice your speech again?" I ask. "You were perfect, Alfie," I tell her. "Only it's '*yellow*,' not '*lellow*.' Remember how you learned to say it? '*Yes, yes,* yellow.'"

"*Yes, yes,* lellow," Alfie repeats, as if she's cooperating with me. "There. Are you happy now, Ell-Way?"

"Sure," I say, sitting down next to her on the fluffy rug.

I'm happy except for the part where I have to tell Mom and Dad what's been going on at school, that is. Let Alfie say her line however she wants—as long as she doesn't wreck the skit. Or embarrass Mom and Dad. "Hey, Alf," I say. "You know what would be fun?" Mr. Bright Idea, here.

"What?"

"A bath," I say. "A *bubble* bath. With lots of toys."

"Go ahead and take one, then," Alfie says, shrugging. "Only don't play with my seahorse."

"I meant *you*," I tell her. **YEESH!**

"I'm busy," Alfie says, and she tugs up the horses' quilt under their chins—if horses even have chins. "Is a fwend coming with you to my *Brown Bear* show?" she asks, looking up. "Like maybe Corey?"

Alfie *loves* Corey. He told her once that her shoes were pretty, and that was it for her.

"He can't come," I say. "He has to get up early the next day, when it's still dark out, because of swimming. So he has to go to bed right after dinner, almost."

"Aw," she says, drooping. "Who wants to swim in the wain?"

That's *"In the rain."*

"I think there's a big roof over the aquatics center," I say. "But I have lots of other friends who might come," I fib. "I was gonna ask Jason Leffer, but—but that didn't work out," I fumble. "He was busy."

Okay, it's a lie, but just a little one. Jason *has* been busy, *trying to avoid me*, ever since the toilet paper thing.

"Huh," Alfie says. *"I see a lellow duck looking at me."*

"Then I thought maybe Diego Romero could come," I say, ignoring the news about the nosy yellow duck. "Only he's already doing something."

Reading, probably. And staying away from kids who wreck library books.

Some recess king *I* turned out to be!

"Huh," Alfie says again. "I don't even know him. But sometimes Suzette and Mona and Arletty are too busy for me, too." She droops even more.

Those are her three best friends at Kreative Learning and Daycare.

"But only *sometimes*," I point out. "Because you play with them a lot. Mostly one at a time."

"I play with Arletty, anyway," Alfie agrees. "She gets to be the green fwog in our play. That big *lucky*."

"That's cool," I say. I'm wondering when I can give up and leave.

Bath or no bath—*I* don't care!

And maybe Mom and Dad have forgotten all about the whole "There's-something-I-have-to-tell-you" thing. Which was my own bright idea, of course.

Another good one, EllRay.

"Alfie-kins," Mom says, popping her head into the room. "Bath's all ready, sweetheart. Come with me."

"But I'm putting my horsies to bed," Alfie says.

I can tell she's not really into the argument, though—and that bath-time will happen in a couple of minutes, tops.

Mom gives me a wink and a thumbs-up as I slip out the door.

✳ 18 ✳

BRAIN SPLINTER

"So, EllRay," Dad says in the family room, his feet propped up in front of him on the long part of the sofa. We are waiting for Mom, who is now trying to get Alfie *out* of the tub, just like I said would happen. "What's up at school? Still leading a rich, full life?"

"I wouldn't say 'rich,'" I begin, thinking of my allowance.

But now's not the time to complain about that, the last logical speck of my brain informs me. Not when there are so many bad things I have to tell him.

In fact, I have *way too much* to tell my mom and dad. The fake TP shortage. The wrecked library book. Us boys fighting during lunch. Well, Mom and Dad might already know about that, thanks to Principal James and his horrible "parents may be notified" threat. In my opinion, that's about ten times worse than yelling, *"I'm gonna tell!"*

I don't think Principal James called, though. That's one good thing. Because if he *had* called, Dad would not be asking, "What's up at school?" He'd be saying, *"What in the world is going on over at Oak Glen Primary School?"* in a very loud voice.

"EllRay?" Dad asks again. "School?"

Okay. Go.

"There have been some problems," I begin, fidgeting in my seat. "Well, *a* problem," I correct myself, thinking of my quest to make at least one new, spare friend by the end of January. I should start with that.

But—instant complication! Because I don't want Dad thinking I'm not popular.

See, that's the whole "brain splinter" thing I was talking about earlier. Like, *my* brain splinter is that I'm the shortest kid in the third grade. And no matter how tall I'm gonna grow later, which Mom and Dad keep promising I will, that doesn't change my shortness now.

1. I can do great on my vocabulary words for the week, but I'm still short.
2. Everyone can laugh at a joke I tell, but I'm still short.
3. I can beat my personal best at *Die, Creature, Die* but I'm still short.

It's always there, like a splinter in my brain.

And, as I said before, my *dad's* brain splinter is that there aren't more brown faces—*families*—around Oak Glen. And he's the one who really wanted us to move here.

So I think one small part of his gigantic brain is always secretly afraid that kids might pick on Alfie and me because our skin is brown.

Well, not afraid. Not Dad. More like *alert.*

But *also* like I said before, and as I have recently proven, there are other reasons for kids to get irked at me.

And Alfie's no picnic either. No offense.

"Finally," Mom says, gliding into the family room. Her clothes are still wet from Alfie's bath. She flings herself onto the other end of the sofa and sighs. "Honestly," she says. "I don't know whether it'll be better or worse when she turns five."

"Probably better," I say, looking on the bright side. I'm about to remind her that *I* turned out pretty well, didn't I? But then I remember why we're all sitting here. "Or maybe not," I say. I grab for a small round pillow and clutch it to my chest like it's a life preserver.

My mom puts little pillows all over the place.

Before even starting to talk again, I decide to skip the making-a-new-friend part of my story. It's too complicated and personal to explain.

I clear my throat. "So, there are three things I want to talk about."

Mom beams a smile in my direction. "Oh, I just love how you're so organized sometimes, EllRay," she says. "You and your lists."

Typical Mom.

"What three things?" my father asks. He is holding very still, probably so that his brain splinter won't start poking him. See, he's already imagining the worst!

Typical Dad.

"Okay," I say. But I feel like I'm sinking to the bottom of a very deep pool, life preserver or no life preserver. "I'll just start. First, there is no toilet paper shortage at Oak Glen Primary School. I never said there *was* one, not really. I just wanted to bring a roll of TP to school for—well, for kind of a joke."

Mom's golden-brown eyes are wide as she takes this in. She is probably picturing the hundreds of rolls of toilet paper she has gotten the other parents to buy. She must also be imagining the embarrassing phone calls she will have to make. "But—but—but—" she sputters.

"You certainly let your mother *think* there was a

shortage," Dad rumbles. Then he turns to my mom. "Obviously, that roll of toilet paper he brought to school was what led to the whole Curse of the Mummy Zombie thing, Louise. But let's let him continue. Go on, son," he says, turning back to me.

Dad just called me "son." I *am* his son, of course, but still, it's not a good sign.

"There's also that library book you let me check out," I say, turning to face Mom. Mom the Merciful, I hope. "I decided to bring it to school," I tell her. "Okay, *sneak* it to school. But I had a really good reason," I add. "And I wrapped the book in aluminum foil so it couldn't even *think* about getting wet. I was taking *really good care of it.*"

"Even though it's against our family rules to bring a library book to school?" Mom asks. "Why, EllRay?"

"Well, I brought it to—to show someone," I say. "Only Ja—I mean, only *this other kid* thought it was gingerbread."

YEESH, I think, starting to sweat a little. I almost gave away Jared's name, after they all stuck up for me yesterday! That's not "flocking together."

And there's no point in getting anyone *else* in trouble around here, is there?

"Gingerbread," Dad repeats, giving me a look.

"I'm not even kidding, Dad," I say. "Gingerbread. And then this strange kid came out of nowhere and grabbed the book from me. And all of a sudden, the whole thing turned into a game of keep-away."

Jared *is* strange. Sometimes, anyway. So that's not a lie.

"Keep-away," Dad says.

I nod. "Only, when the guy found out the book *wasn't* gingerbread, it fell on the ground," I try to explain. "By accident. I don't know, it happened really fast. But I'll pay the library back," I say. "Every penny."

By now, Mom and Dad are just staring at me. "Is that it?" Dad finally asks.

"Only one more thing," I tell him. I mean them. "There was kind of a fake fight after the book accidentally fell in the mud."

"How do you have a fake fight?" Mom asks. She looks confused.

"A bunch of us *were* mad at each other," I admit.

I am trying to be as honest as I can. Well, almost. "And we were kind of *pretending* we were gonna fight. But then some big kids saw us, and started yelling, 'Fight, fight!' So we really had to. Fight, I mean."

"Who's 'we'?" Dad asks.

"Oh, most of us boys," I say, not wanting to be a tattle-tale. "But a lot of them were on my side. Corey, Kevin, and Nate. Major and Marco."

"Marco Adair?" my mom asks. "I met his mother at Visitor's Day. What a lovely woman."

"Yeah, Marco's really nice, too," I agree. "He's been sticking up for me a lot, lately, come to think of it."

"But you guys didn't have to fight," Dad informs me. "This was all about the library book, and nothing more? Because somehow, I'm not buying it."

Brain splinter.

And "I'm not buying it" means he thinks I'm lying. Or at least leaving something out, which I am. But it's not what he thinks.

"I guess the fight was also because the book wasn't gingerbread," I say, trying to remember. "It's kind of hard to explain."

"Apparently so," Dad says. "So is *that* it?"

"That's it," I say.

That's it until tomorrow, anyway. Until my next goof-up.

Dad runs his hands back through what is left of his hair. "I'd like to hear the part of the story you're leaving out, son," he says after one long, quiet minute.

"But I'm not—"

"Because *why* would you suddenly change from good old reliable EllRay Jakes into this—this absolute *gold mine* of bad ideas?" he asks. "In just the last two or three days? Swiping household supplies," he begins, like he's reading from a list. "Making a mess on the playground. Disobeying family rules about library books. Ruining public property. And getting goaded into a lunch-time brawl by a bunch of yahoos."

"I didn't *swipe* the toilet paper," I remind him. "I asked Mom, and she said yes."

"EllRay," Dad says. "What is going on?"

I think my mom is holding her breath. I can't even look at her.

"I—I only wanted to make another friend," I

manage to say, finally spitting out the truth. "A spare," I mumble. "So I came up with my recess king plan."

"Your recess king plan," Dad says. He is turning into an echo chamber tonight.

"But honey," Mom says to me. "You already have *lots* of friends."

"No offense, but you only think that because you're my mom," I inform her. "I have exactly one-and-a-half good, solid friends," I say. "Corey, and half of Kevin. Except Corey's busy with swimming most of the time. And me not having enough friends isn't setting a very good example for Alfie, is it?" I ask, the words spilling out of me now.

"What does *Alfie* have to do with any of this?" Dad asks, frowning big-time.

"She wanted me to bring a friend to her show tomorrow night," I try to explain. "And I couldn't think of anyone."

"Oh," Mom says. She—frowns, thinking.

"Other kids have *lots* of friends, Mom," I inter-rupt. "Tons of them. And no," I say, turning to face my dad. "*This is not because I have brown skin.*

Or because I'm short," I add, surprising myself. "I guess it's because I'm *me*."

Wow. Does that make things worse, or what?

"I don't understand where this is coming from," Mom says. "You get along with everyone, EllRay. Most of the time, at least. And everyone gets along with you. Believe me, I would have heard about it, otherwise."

"And no," Dad chimes in. "Other kids do *not* all have 'tons of friends,' as you put it. In fact, I think just about every kid in the world thinks other kids are swimming in friends." He shrugs. "And as I just told you, the answer is no, they aren't."

Huh, I think, wondering if what he just said could possibly be true. "I don't want to *swim* in friends," I tell him. "I just want a couple of spares, that's all."

"To set a good example for Alfie," Dad says, repeating my earlier words.

Does he think I'm lying?

"Look. Everyone's tired," Dad says. "We can sort out all these incidents over the weekend, after things have calmed down around here."

"Can't I just find out my punishment now?" I ask. "And get that part over with? Or I won't be able to sleep."

"Tell you what," Dad says. He gets to his feet in a that's-that kind of way. "You start thinking about how you're going to earn the money to pay for, say, half the cost of that library book. That ought to keep you busy for a while. And no more wacky recess king schemes, okay?"

I nod, hiding a sigh.

"EllRay, listen," Mom says. "I've got an idea. What about asking that boy Marco to come over tomorrow night. He sounds like someone you'd have fun with.

And she's right. I think I *would* have fun with Marco. He's been really nice to me lately.

1. Marco tried to tell Ms. Sanchez that the grass wasn't all that dirty when little Iggy collapsed on the ground during the zombie fiasco.

2. He shared his mini muffins with me at recess— and his dragons, too.

3. He even stood up for me in Principal James's office.

Why didn't I think of Marco before now? Just because he's friends with Major doesn't mean he can't be friends with me, too!

"You could call him, EllRay," Mom says. "I have their number in the other room. Call him now and invite him to spend the night tomorrow. We'll have a ball, I promise. I can talk to Mrs. Adair after you talk to him and we can work out the details."

"Just don't tell him he's Marco-Adair-the-Spare," Dad advises. "You should keep that little nugget to yourself."

Which I will.

"Okay," I say, bouncing to my feet like an EllRay cloud that just got lifted up by a gust of wind.

Because—*dude*.

Marco might be coming over!

* 19 *

BRAND-NEW EYES

"Hey, Alfie," I say in the back seat of the car the next morning on the way to school. "I'm bringing a friend to your show tonight."

"Shh. I'm busy pwacticing inside my bwain," Alfie says, scowling.

That's *"practicing inside my brain."* Rehearsing her one line.

"Don't you want to know who I'm bringing?" I ask. "I'll tell you his nickname," I whisper, "It's 'the armpit noise king.'" And I make the noise with my tongue and lips as quietly as I can.

"Eww," Alfie says, but she's smiling big.

And I thought liking stuff like that was just a guy thing! I guess four-year-olds get it, too. "And you're bwinging Corey?" Alfie asks.

"I already told you, he can't come," I say. "This is a new friend."

I like the sound of those words. *"A new friend."* Just like I planned.

Okay, maybe not *exactly* as I planned—or even close, really. Because as of today, Friday, both Jason Leffer and Diego Romero are farther away from wanting to hang with me than ever before.

But that might change some day. You never know!

And Marco counts, doesn't he?

Just because I didn't plan it this way doesn't mean it's not cool!

"I see a lellow duck looking at me," Alfie says.

"That's 'yellow,'" I say. "Remember? *'Yes, yes, yellow.'"*

"EllRay," Mom warns from the front seat as she nears Kreative Learning and Daycare. "Okay, Miss Alfie," she says a minute later, sounding cheerful and matter-of-fact as can be. "Out you hop."

"That's *Arletty* who gets to hop," Alfie grumbles as I help her with the seatbelt. "Because she's the frog. That lucky."

"Now, I'm picking you up at two-thirty, remember," Mom tells Alfie, quickly changing the subject. She's had a lot of practice doing that. "We'll dash home for a fabulous snack," Mom continues. "And then you can take a rest before the big show."

"Where's her costume?" I ask, looking around the back seat.

"I turned it in yesterday afternoon," Mom half whispers, getting out of the car. "Miss Nancy is really on top of things this year," she adds as she opens Alfie's door.

"But she's not the boss of me," Alfie says, scrambling out of her car seat.

"Actually, she is," I point out. "At school, anyway."

Alfie had better not make that mistake at Oak Glen Primary School next year!

"Alfie knows that," Mom tells me, laughing as she straightens my sister's little pink jacket. She tweaks Alfie's braids. "She's only teasing, EllRay."

But I'm not so sure.

Tonight might be more entertaining than Mom and Dad are thinking it will be.

It's like I am looking around Oak Glen Primary School with brand-new eyes as I walk onto the sunny playground this morning.

Maybe it's because I don't know what's going to happen today!

I have no secret goal. I am not trying to move other kids around like checkers, making them want to be friends with me. There's just—*right now.*

It's a very relaxing feeling.

I already learned this week that *bad* things can happen even if you think you have made a really good plan. **SURPRISE!**

But now, I know that *good* things can also happen without me having to come up with some goofy scheme—like my brilliant recess king idea.

Marco Adair wants to be friends with me. I didn't even have to trick him into it!

"Hi, EllRay," Corey shouts from way over by the playground shed. It looks like he has been showing off his mad paddleboard skills to Major. Luckily, Mr. Hale is busy at the swings, where someone—Little Miss Nosebleed again?—is having an emergency.

"Hi," I yell. I toss my backpack onto one of the boys' picnic tables. **THUNK!**

I look around with my new eyes. Diego and Nate are huddled together at the end of another picnic table. They are probably talking about cars.

Well, why not? They both like 'em.

I'm not even jealous.

Well, not *very*.

Behind the picnic tables, Jared, Kevin, and Stanley are hanging from the chain-link fence like bats, only not upside-down. Jared is higher than the other two, of course. But so what? Jared likes to be the boss, and I guess Kevin and Stanley don't mind being bossed. Every so often, anyway.

Me, not so much.

But it's like that with us guys. We're different from the girls in my class. They can take sides, hold grudges, and have invisible wars for days, and not even Ms. Sanchez knows what's going on.

With us boys, though, our friendships shape-shift and change the way my robotic insect action figure turns into a tank, then back into an attack bug again. And we're all pretty cool together, no matter how the shape-shifting comes out.

It's such a *relief,* being a boy and not a girl!

From now on, I'll have a new friend to do stuff with when Corey and Kevin are busy. And Major can hang, too, if he wants. And Corey, and Kevin. I like them all.

"Win-win," as my dad would say.

"Hey, EllRay," Marco calls out as he bounces onto the playground and heads toward me. "I brought some stuff to show you," he hollers. He looks around like a not-very-good secret agent.

But Mr. Havens is still busy over at the swings.

"Watcha got?" I ask, going over to meet him halfway.

And it's really okay if it's the plastic knights again, I remind myself. I can always teach him how to play *Die, Creature, Die* some other time.

Like—tonight!

✳ 20 ✳

WHAT DO YOU SEE?

The big room at Kreative Learning and Daycare is kind of rowdy during the pause before the last part of the show, Alfie's skit. We have already made it through the two-year-olds' songs, "The Itsy-Bitsy Spider," "Heads, Shoulders, Knees and Toes," and "If You're Happy and You Know It." Those three songs took a surprisingly long time.

In fact, it already feels like tomorrow.

Then we watched the three-year-olds' performance of "The Gingerbread Man," read aloud by Miss Nancy herself.

Gingerbread? It's following me around!

I half expected Jared to come bursting through the door, demanding his share.

And now it's almost Alfie's turn. Dad is checking something on his cell, but Mom looks nervous as the voices around us grow louder.

I give Marco a look. "Dude," I tell him. "Noisy, huh? And wait until you meet Alfie after the show. She's like the *princess* of noisy. She's gonna be the red bird in this skit," I explain in advance.

"The red bird," Marco says, like he's memorizing it.

"She wanted to be the goldfish, but it didn't work out," I explain.

"Huh," Marco says. He looks confused.

I think maybe he's an only child.

"Let's get this show on the road," a dad behind me says, and his wife shushes him.

"*Hello, everyone,*" Miss Nancy calls out again from the stage, which is really just the back part of the room marked off by blue tape. She claps her hands a few times to get our attention, and everyone in the audience settles down.

"Oh, here we go," Mom whispers. Dad puts away his cell.

Miss Nancy clears her throat, and the microphone squeals. "Next, we have our four-year-olds' spirited version of that beloved children's book, *Brown Bear, Brown Bear, What Do You See?* The book was written by Bill Martin Junior, and illustrated by Eric Carle," she says. "And here's our cast!"

The four-year-olds march out dressed in their costumes. My dad nods his approval of Alfie's fluttering red feathers and yellow beak-nose. He gives Mom a thumbs-up. Everyone cheers and claps.

I clap too, because this might be as good as it gets.

I know this book very well. It goes through a whole bunch of animals seeing each other. Nine of them, Mom said. It ends with the last one—the goldfish Alfie wanted to be—seeing the teacher, who then sees all the kids.

In this skit, Mom told me that Miss Nancy is going to read the first line of the verse for each animal, asking, "What do you see?" Then the kids are supposed to say they see the next animal, and so on. It's better than I'm making it sound.

Miss Nancy clears her throat, then she asks the kid playing the brown bear what he sees. And unfortunately, when the bear steps up to the microphone, he says he sees the red bird. Alfie.

Then Miss Nancy asks the red bird what *she* sees.

And Alfie just stands there, staring out at the audience. Her eyes are huge.

It's as if my little sister didn't realize anyone would be watching the skit—even though she said she wanted to be the goldfish so she'd get all the clapping!

It feels like everyone in the audience is holding their breath.

Marco nudges me. "Dude," he whispers. "Is Fluffy supposed to be doing that?"

"It's Alfie, not Fluffy. And *nuh-uh*," I whisper back.

On the stage, Miss Nancy is nodding her head at Alfie, encouraging her to say her one line so the show can go on. So everyone can go home tonight. I can tell the teacher is about to repeat the opening question—which will not help Alfie one little bit.

I know my sister, see.

This is going to end in tears, or with a public meltdown. Either way, the next couple of weeks are going to be a disaster around our house.

Alfie might be small, but her temper is large.

The audience is murmuring now, but anything anyone does will only make things worse.

Almost anything.

"Do it," I tell Marco, giving him a look.

"Do what?"

"Your armpit thing. And *quick*," I whisper.

"You mean it?" Marco asks. He looks like he's about to faint.

"Hurry," I say, nodding. "Don't even think about it. Just do it."

Luckily, Marco already took off his jacket. And he is wearing a short-sleeved T-shirt.

He wipes his hands on his pants. Then he makes a cup shape with one hand and slides it under the opposite shirt sleeve. He puts it really tight over his armpit, with no air holes allowed, he told me once. He bends that arm, lifting it up like a chicken wing. And then really fast, he lowers his elbow, flattening the cupped hand.

FLIRRRRPPT!

The armpit noise echoes throughout the room. It's like it's bouncing off the walls and onto the stage! Alfie jumps as if she just got a shock—and then she starts to laugh.

She knows it was Marco! *She's looking right at us!*

Corey had better watch his back, because I think Marco's her hero, now.

And I'm not jealous, even one little bit.

"That boy's full of surprises," Dad murmurs to Mom, who has both hands over her face.

"He's full of *something*," she mumbles through her fingers.

Alfie strides up to the microphone, flaps her fluffy red wings, and says her line nice and loud. *"I see a yellow duck looking at me!"*

No baby talk "lellow." No whispering into the microphone. It was *perfect*.

Yay, Alfie!

She steps back and bows.

And everyone claps and cheers again, this time just for her!

The show can't continue until things calm down.

Mom and Dad still look like they're in shock, after that astounding **FLIRRRRPPT**. But basically, if Alfie's happy, they're happy.

And Alfie is definitely happy.

"Thumbs up, dog," I say, giving my talented new friend Marco a nudge in the ribs—and a great big smile. "I owe you one."

"Nah. We're good," Marco says, grinning back at me.

And I realize that the remainder of the skit, and tonight—and the whole rest of the semester, for that matter—are gonna go great.

I just know it!

STAY TUNED FOR THE NEXT ELLRAY
ADVENTURE IN EARLY 2016!